Books By Tahir Shah

SCORPION SOUP

A Story in a Story

TAHIR SHAH

SCORPION SOUP

A Story in a Story

TAHIR SHAH

SECRETUM MUNDI PUBLISHING

MMXX

Secretum Mundi Publishing Ltd
Kemp House
City Road
London
EC1V 2NX
United Kingdom

www.secretum-mundi.com
info@secretum-mundi.com

First published, 2013
Secretum Mundi Publishing edition, 2020
VERSION 09112020

SCORPION SOUP

© TAHIR SHAH

Visit the author's website at:

tahirshah.com

ISBN 978-1-912383-70-2

Descend down through the layers
of an onion's skin and you will find
true wisdom.

Afghan saying

This book is dedicated
to the memory of my grandfather,
The Sirdar Ikbal Ali Shah –
Savant, Storyteller, and Man of Men.

CONTENTS

Introduction

WHEN I WAS small I was told stories from morning till night.

I was told stories about genies and witches and about great birds that could carry away elephants on their wings... and stories about distant kingdoms and magical lands ruled by warrior kings.

I was told stories of good and bad... and stories of hope and others of despair.

I was even told stories about stories.

And all the while, I listened, amazed.

The more I listened, the more my mind worked. And the more I came to understand that these stories had a power about them, a secret lifeblood all of their own.

They were magical instruments, machineries that could alter states of mind and change the way we think.

Stories are part of the default programming of Man. They are within us all, born into us, and they make us who we are – they make us human.

Since earliest childhood, I have feasted on these stories, especially those contained in *The Thousand and One Nights*.

A treasury of storytelling and culture that is in itself a labyrinth of worlds, *The Nights* conjures realms more fantastical than any I know.

What I like best is when there are tales concealed within tales – interwoven, complex, mesmerizing to the senses and the soul.

To descend down through the layers of stories is to be reborn, into a dominion of fantasy, one touched by real magic.

Scorpion Soup is a small hymn to *The Thousand and One Nights*... and to the stories that have made me who I am.

Tahir Shah

The Fisherman

WHEN I WAS young and foolish, but so certain I was wise, I took any work offered.

Sometimes I toiled days at a stretch without ever sleeping – cleaning fish, bailing water from flimsy craft, scrubbing filth from the decks. And at other times I would lose myself in strange lands, listen to the tales that sailors so like to tell, and would think of the love I had left a world away at home.

The years passed.

Look at my hands and you will see I tell you the truth. My palms are coarse and callused, tattooed with adventure and with the trials of fate.

Frequently, I promised myself to quit the life of roaming, to settle down in Haifa, where my family was from. But each time I reached my own port, I was talked into embarking on yet one more journey.

And another.

Then, one night in the month of August, my fishing vessel was wrecked during a violent summer gale off the coast of North Africa. The only survivor, I was captured and taken prisoner by a band of Barbary pirates.

Nothing pleased them more than gaining another seaman for nothing, a lost soul to barter in the slave market at Oran.

They had in their party thirty others already. Each one a rough sea dog scraped up from Barbary shores; each just enough alive to coax a ransom.

Day after day after day we marched, dawn until dusk.

One foot after the other, as the dreaded destination of Oran inched closer. And, each day, we appreciated a little more the freedom we had once known, but hadn't realized that we possessed.

Weeks passed, and the wretched captives descended towards Hell. It came one night in the shape of the cells at the infamous Oran death camp. No description, however wanton, could do justice to that place.

We were trussed up in a long stone barrack in

the dark. Emaciated bundles of sinew and bone, we were chained together in rows of a dozen and a half. The dead were left where they had expired. Only when their putrefied flesh was quite rotten were they removed, their bones pulled from the manacles like a roasted chicken.

I languished there for months, quite certain I would never see the light of day again. I prayed for God to take me, to release me.

And I gave up all hope.

But, one night, the captive beside me murmured a mouthful of words.

I dared not reply or greet him. For the jailer had a habit of severing the windpipes of innocent men if he heard so much as a whisper coming from the cells.

In no more than the faintest mumble, he recounted a tale.

And it was by that tale's sustenance that I survived…

Idyll

IN HEAT MORE terrible than I can describe, we sailed into a small cove far to the south – a cove nestled on the coastline of far-off Senegal.

We went ashore, slung hammocks in the trees, built a fire on the beach, and cooked up some langoustines.

I can taste their meat now: all juicy and tender, a hint of coconut and spice.

That cove was idyllic, a paradise known only to one who has courted the sea. Close my eyes and I see the shadows thrown by the palm fronds in late afternoon, and I hear the sound of the birds chirruping in the heat.

As the evening approached, we sat round and shared stories, stories of our travels and of our lives.

I remember it, clear as I am here with you now.

The man beside me was a Spaniard. His name

was Alfonso, and he had one of those faces you could never forget: hollow features and an expression baked through from ordeal and tribulation.

Drawing a little on his pipe, he stooped forwards to stoke the fire for a moment, his eyes lost in memory.

'I will tell you a tale,' he said softly. 'A tale of another time, a time when I was not a sailor, but an apprentice to a master bookbinder, in Toledo. The bookbinder was the greatest craftsman of his age, from a family of ancestral binders to royalty, no less. Clients would arrive at his workshop from across Spain. Sometimes they even came from France, and beyond. And it was a Frenchman, a famous writer from Troyes, with whom this tale is concerned...'

Capilongo

ONE DAY THE French writer made a special journey to Toledo to meet the master bookbinder.

He arrived by appointment as he always did. For days before his arrival, the apprentices polished and cleaned the workshop, and laid out the finest leathers and samples of the very best work.

On the morning that the writer was due to come, there was a great sense of expectation. We put on our best clothes, polished our shoes until they shone like silver, and greased back our hair with lavender pomade.

At a little after ten, a lacquered carriage pulled up in front of the workshop. The bookbinder, whose name was Fernandez, swept up to the door and opened it wide. Greeting the author with deep respect, he invited him in.

Under the Frenchman's arm was a handwritten manuscript.

It was not so big, about the size of a prayer book, but was printed on very fine paper. Each folio was watermarked with the author's crest, and had an uneven deckle edge.

The writer explained to señor Fernandez that the manuscript was very important indeed. It was his masterwork, and was to be a gift destined for the Pope. Accordingly, the volume was to be bound in the very best leather, the title embossed with the most expensive gold leaf.

For an hour or more the author went over the details, the exact method of binding that was to be used. He said that price and time were no object. The most superlative materials were to be sought out and used, and only the master craftsman himself was to work on the binding.

When señor Fernandez enquired how long he would be given to complete the task, the writer shrugged.

'Take all the time you require,' he said. 'But remember that I am expecting the best work of your life!'

With that, the French author opened a briefcase and removed a purse filled with gold coins. After he had poured them onto the bookbinder's palm, the two men shook hands.

A moment later, the writer was gone.

As soon as he had left, my master collapsed onto a chair and thrust his head into his hands.

'Where will I get a piece of leather worthy of this manuscript?' he asked, over and over.

I motioned at the swatches on display.

'None of them will do, you fool!' the bookbinder cried. 'Don't offer me coal when I am in need of a diamond!'

A few days passed, and then weeks, and months.

Señor Fernandez slipped into a terrible depression. He began to drink heavily, and we feared he had forgotten about the French author's commission altogether. Whenever any of the apprentices mentioned it, the craftsman would fly into a rage and bawl at us. Without the right leather, he declared that he could never begin.

Then, one morning in September, señor Fernandez was reading a letter from a correspondent at his desk when, suddenly, he leapt to his feet. Waving the paper in the air, his face gripped with mania, he yelled:

'*This* is the answer! *This* is the answer!'

The apprentices gathered round.

I took the paper and read aloud from the bottom of the page:

'A new species of mammal has been seen for the first time in the Spice Islands. It has been named the "Capilongo", and it is a cross between a boar and a bird, with the hands of a monkey, and with the intelligence of a human child. No one has yet managed to catch the Capilongo alive.'

The old bookbinder instructed his apprentices to line up and to clear their minds. We did so, and he then asked for a volunteer – for a man sufficiently brave or foolhardy to go and capture the Capilongo. Only the creature's leather would do, he insisted, for the manuscript destined for the Pope.

No one volunteered.

One by one, the apprentices stepped back in fear. After all, they were bookbinders, not explorers. Unsure quite why, I leant forward, no more than an inch or two, but it was enough.

'I will do it,' I said in less than a whisper. 'I will go and capture the jungle beast and bring back its hide.'

The next day I set off.

I travelled first to Constantinople, and from there by sailing ship, dhow and hollowed-out canoe, until I reached the pristine waters of the Spice Islands. Never has an adventurer embarked on a journey with less preparation or know-how than I.

Until then, I was a raw page waiting for a story of its own.

All I knew was that the Capilongo was out there, somewhere, and that if I could hunt it, capture it, and take its hide, then there would be a smile on the lips of an old bookbinder, a writer, and possibly the Pope as well.

The voyage was uncomfortable in the extreme.

But, in my untested condition, I hardly knew the meaning of the word – *discomfort*. Had I any inkling of what was to come, I would have savoured the weeks I spent upon turbulent seas.

The one meeting of interest was with a missionary who was drunk from one dawn to the next. He was accompanying a shipment of Bibles, printed in Cintra. He told me that they were destined for tattooed savages.

'Where are they, the savages?' I asked.

'Deep in the jungle,' came the reply.

After a great many deviations, the vessel docked at a ramshackle port. I descended the gangplank onto the quay, the name of a mythical creature filling my head and my mouth. With no idea how to proceed, I followed the bales of Bibles destined for savages.

There is no feeling quite so contrary as arriving in a foreign land, with no grasp of language or etiquette. The heat was the first thing that hit me, dead straight between the eyes.

The bales of Bibles were unloaded by sweat-drenched stevedores and hauled in fits and starts towards that terrible seething undergrowth.

And I followed them.

The missionary bought a bottle of homemade liquor, quaffed it down, and thanked God for protecting him.

'Pray to the Lord so that you, too, might be blessed,' he said caustically. 'Neglect the Saviour, and the Angel of Death will be your shadow.'

Draining the bottle, he reeled about.

'The jungle...' he said after a long pause, rolling the word off his tongue as if it were a bitter olive, 'it will swallow you whole, devour you, crush your bones to dust.'

We progressed on wagons and on mule carts, on hollowed-out logs, and skiffs, until at last the precious cargo was unloaded on the banks of a great russet-brown river. It was all murky and warm, like bathwater left through a long sultry afternoon, and it stank of both life and death.

The missionary drank another bottle of liquor.

Then another... and declared that the Word of the Lord would be the salvation of the savages.

I asked him again where they were, the savage peoples of whom he spoke so often and with such trepidation. Raising a fist out before him, he pointed at the trees.

'They live on the Mountains of Medusa,' he said.

With no other plan having presented itself, I tagged along, in the hope that the savages would in turn lead me to the elusive Capilongo.

A team of porters was hired.

The Bibles and supplies having been laden onto their backs, we set out from the river and into the forest canopy.

After a few minutes of staggering under loads, we found ourselves in a fearful realm of nature. The towering trees reminded us of our frailty.

The creepers and the vines tripped us, the chorus of unfamiliar sounds haunted each step.

The missionary kept the porters content with a ration of dates in honey. But it soon ran out. When it did so, he resorted to a whip.

Any man who refused to pull his weight was lashed to the bone.

Each night we slung hammocks, squeezed water from oversized tubular flowers, and we prayed.

The missionary prayed that the Bibles would reach the savages, and I prayed that I would find the Capilongo, smite it, and return to my master with its skin.

The porters had never ventured into the undergrowth before. They spent their lives down at the river and said that only a madman would wish to trek towards the hinterland. When I asked them about the Mountains of Medusa, they seemed to shake with fear. Then, one morning, the missionary and I awoke to find ourselves alone.

The porters had absconded, and they had taken the supplies with them. The only thing they left was the Bibles. We called out, our voices lost in the trees.

'We can try and retrace our steps to the river,' I said limply.

The missionary spat at the idea. He opened one of the boxes and removed half a dozen of the Bibles. They were well bound in indigo buckram with silver lettering down the spine.

'The savages need the Word of the Lord,' he said firmly, 'and so I will go on.'

'You will die,' I replied.

The missionary smiled at my remark, smoothed a hand down over his grey beard and said,

'The Lord is my protector and my guide.'

With that, he turned on his heel and moved boisterously into the undergrowth, clutching an armful of the holy books.

I stood there in silence for a long time, unsure of what to do. There would have been safety in numbers, but the missionary was hell-bent on suicide. Without food or equipment, he had no hope of survival, with or without the Word of the Lord.

Standing there, the jungle encroaching around me, I was suddenly overcome with a vision. In my mind's eye I glimpsed a great and unwieldy creature with the snout of a pig and the feathers of a bird. Poised erect on two feet, taller than a man, it appeared to have a very singular presence. As I watched the hallucination, the creature, what I supposed to be the Capilongo, opened a leather bag, removed a book, and began to read.

I blinked, and the vision was gone.

For seven days and nights I waited there at the same spot, the emerald canopy pressing ever closer, hunger gnawing at my ribs. I survived by squeezing water from the tubular flowers, and by eating the berries of the low shrubs that were common on the forest floor. I might have retraced my steps down to the river, but I had no idea in which direction it lay.

Something inside me was telling me to wait.

So I did.

And then, on the seventh night, the vision came again.

This time, the Capilongo was not reading, but smoking a pipe, staring into the embers of a dying fire. As I watched, he narrowed his eyes, and he whispered:

'Dear apprentice, I know you are watching me. And I am waiting for you.'

Then, as if answering my unspoken question, he added:

'Follow the golden bird.'

At dawn the next day, I was woken by the shrill sound of a tiny bird, no bigger than a hummingbird. It was hovering beside my face, as if it were hoping to gain my attention. Rubbing my eyes, I saw that it wished for me to follow it. I jumped up and, before I knew it, was running through the jungle in pursuit of the golden bird.

I chased and chased, the tangle of vines and twisted branches hampering each footstep. The little bird seemed to understand that I was an unfamiliar visitor to its jungle. Floundering about clumsily, I wished for wings to take to the air as he. From time to time, he would hover beside me, allowing me to catch my breath, before hurrying on.

By the night of the first day I reached a glade of empty ground.

Pinned out in the centre of it was the headless body of a man. Even before I had drawn near, I had guessed its identity. For all around it were torn pages, the Word of the Lord.

I buried the missionary under a pile of flat-sided stones, and read a passage from Genesis over him. I ought to have had fear, because his head was missing – chopped off, I imagined, by savages.

But for the first time since my departure from Toledo, I had hope.

Through three more days I chased the golden bird, until the air became cool and free from the insects that plagued my waking hours. I crouched on the banks of a little stream, chewed a handful of berries, and fell back with surprise.

Standing over me was the Capilongo.

'Excuse me for startling you,' he said in a polite voice.

I breathed in hard, choking in surprise.

The Capilongo reached down and offered me his hand. It was soft, covered in chocolate-brown feathers.

'I saw you in a dream,' I said.

'And I saw you,' the Capilongo replied, 'and I know why you have come.'

Glancing at the ground, I mumbled the word 'duty'.

'Before you kill me,' said the Capilongo, 'please do me the honour of dining with me. You see, I have very little chance to make intelligent conversation.'

I agreed readily. After all, it was the least I could do.

The creature led me to a cave behind the stream. It was gigantic, carpeted in scented moss and illuminated by shafts of natural light. Arranged down the middle was a long banquet table, at which two places had been laid at one end.

Welcoming me to his home, the Capilongo ushered me to the head of the table, and clapped his hands.

Nothing happened, not for a moment at least.

Then, slowly, an army of sloths slipped from the shadows, their long, curved arms laden with dishes and plates.

We dined on wild fruits, the seeds of which looked like cut diamonds, on slivers of raw blue meat, and on a kind of jelly that smelled of frogs. The sloth servants ferried one dish after another to the table.

I asked if there were savages living near. The Capilongo looked up sharply.

'There is a tribe up in the mountains,' he said, reaching for a segment of fruit. 'They live on the brains of their vanquished foes. The skulls are stored beneath the ground in vats, pickled for months in the juice from the lowreeh tree.'

'Do they hunt Capilongos?' I asked.

My host sniffed.

'I am pleased to report that they do not,' he said.

Before I could reply, the Capilongo reached down and picked up a knife. An assassin's dagger of sorts, it had a sharp point and a long, straight shaft. He turned it carefully so that the blade was held in his fingers, the hilt pointing towards my chest.

'Capilongos have two traditions,' he said in a kindly tone. 'The first is always to assist a guest in anything he might require. The second is to entertain an assassin before he carries out his duty. This knife is sharp enough to stab me easily in the heart, or to slit my throat, whichever you prefer. But, before you dispatch me,' said the Capilongo earnestly, 'I would ask that you permit me a small indulgence.'

Wondering what it was, I nodded.

'Of course.'

'Would you mind me regaling you with a story?

Think of it as an entertainment, a parting gift.'

I could hardly believe what I was hearing. But, delighted at having arrived at my quarry so easily, I accepted.

The Capilongo clapped his hands and the sloth servants cleared the plates.

When the serving dishes were gone, an elderly sloth glided over to the table. Between his upturned hands was held a salver, a bottle of aged jungle brandy upon it. When two glasses of the tawny liquid had been poured, the Capilongo lit his pipe and his tale began…

Mittle-Mittle

THERE WAS ONCE a kingdom in the Horn of Africa where all the men were brave, and all the women were beautiful.

Surrounded by desert, it was a land of great abundance and verdure. The grass was the colour of crushed emeralds, the flowers dazzling pinks, reds and blues, and the air crystal clear.

At one end of the land there was a mountain capped all year round with blinding white snow and, at the other, a forest impenetrable and dark – the Forest of Empty Souls.

There was no king, because the people had found over centuries that they did better without a leader. The last king had passed away without issue, and it was then that the citizens decided they didn't have any need of a monarch at all.

When there was a matter to be dealt with or decided, they went to a pool in the palace, a pool filled with toads. And, with great reverence, they consulted the toads.

Although no one in the kingdom could speak the language of the toads, they found that the creatures seemed to understand what they were being asked. Through croaking and twitches of their wart-covered bodies, the amphibians managed to make their feelings known.

Now, in the kingdom there was a special shrine. There was no religion as such, yet the shrine was worshipped night and day, and revered like nothing else.

A thousand and one steps crafted from porphyry led up to the central chamber. Each morning and each night it was rinsed with tears gathered from the populace.

As there was no sadness, or very little indeed, the people grew a special kind of onion, the mere hint of which made their eyes stream with tears. Enormous fields of these onions were grown by the farmers, for the sole purpose of rinsing the steps of the sacred shrine. The women would take it in turns weeping into miniature silver buckets, which were taken ceremoniously to the steps at dusk and at dawn.

As for the shrine, the interior walls were fashioned from pure gold, embossed with the images of toads at play. Deep inside, beyond a golden screen of filigree, lay a simple chamber. And in the chamber was a plinth, on which stood a cedarwood box the colour of walnuts, all cracked with age.

No one in the kingdom had ever seen the contents of the box. It's not that they didn't want to, rather that they were so fearful that no one had ever dared to open it.

From time to time children, as they drifted to sleep, would ask their mothers what was in the shrine.

The answer was always the same:

'There is a box, my dear.'

'But what's in it?'

Every mother in the land always gave the same reply:

'Never you mind. Go to sleep now and leave it at that.'

One day, a boy of about eight or nine found that he couldn't stop thinking about the box.

His name was Mittle-Mittle, which meant 'good-hearted' in the language of the kingdom. He begged and begged, and he begged and begged, but his mother refused to reveal anything more than she knew – that in the sacred shrine was a box, a box the colour of walnuts, all cracked with age.

Disgruntled at getting a less than satisfactory answer to his question, Mittle-Mittle decided to venture to the shrine and have a look for himself.

The next morning, when all the other little boys were huddled over their desks in school, Mittle-Mittle slipped unnoticed through the streets, passed the Toad Palace, and scampered up the great long staircase, just as it had been deluged in a rinsing of fresh tears.

The guards didn't notice the boy because they wore special helmets which made seeing anything shorter than themselves very difficult indeed.

With care and on tiptoes, Mittle-Mittle zigzagged his way through the gold-walled chambers, until he came to the room in which the box was kept.

At that very moment, his mother was chopping onions and blinking into a silver bucket, quite unaware that her favourite son was up to no good. But the last thing on Mittle-Mittle's mind was his mother, and the part she played in the tradition of the land.

As he entered the chamber in which the box was kept, the boy wiped a hand down over his mouth and glanced around carefully, making certain he wasn't about to be caught. No one seemed to be watching, and so, very quietly, he crept forwards until he was standing beside the box.

The keyhole was in line with his lips.

Reaching up, he prised the lid open, his small fingers forcing the hinges apart.

He craned forwards, straining on tiptoes, holding his breath.

'Oh,' said Mittle-Mittle in a whisper. 'I see.'

A few inches away in the box, laid on a bed of dusty green felt, was a nail.

It was rusty, bent at one end, and appeared to be very old. Without thinking, Mittle-Mittle snatched up the nail.

Leaving the lid of the box wide open, he hurried away backwards, so that if anyone saw him they would imagine he was arriving rather than on his way out.

In his bedroom that night, Mittle-Mittle made a careful inspection of the nail. But, after a considerable amount of examination, even with a scratched magnifying glass, he came to the conclusion that there was nothing unusual about it at all.

As he regarded it again, his mother slipped in to kiss him goodnight. Her face was fraught with worry, her eyes red from weeping.

'A terrible thing has happened,' she said.

Mittle-Mittle asked her what.

'The sacred box in the sacred shrine has been opened, and its contents have been stolen! The entire kingdom is in disarray. Every home is being searched by the guards, and every woman is weeping a little extra, to rinse the sacred steps that have been so unpardonably defiled.'

'But how can the guards find what is missing if they don't know what was in the box in the first place?'

Mittle-Mittle's mother frowned.

'They will know,' she said decisively. 'Believe me, they will know.'

When his mother had tucked him in bed and was gone, the boy opened the window a crack. He was about to toss the nail out, when he had an idea. He had often heard his father talk of a wise man that lived in the dark, impenetrable Forest of

Empty Souls – a wise man who wore an amulet made from a dodo's skull.

The wise man would know why there was an ordinary nail kept in the box.

Slipping on his clothes, Mittle-Mittle climbed through the window, the old nail clutched tight in his palm. He hurried through the empty streets until he was at the edge of town.

A little further, and he found himself at the forest.

Most other boys might have felt a pang of fear in their gut, but Mittle-Mittle wasn't fearful of anything at all. Slinking between the trees, he snaked his way towards the middle of the forest where he expected the wise man to live.

Meanwhile, in the town, the guards were searching from house to house, questioning one family after another. Eventually they arrived at Mittle-Mittle's home. The boy's father opened the door to them courteously, inviting them in. A moment later, their son's empty bed was discovered, the window open.

Mittle-Mittle's parents were dragged away to the cells.

Deep in the Forest of Empty Souls, an elderly

man was huddled over a fire at the base of a towering green winter oak. With eyes closed, he was murmuring incantations, scribbling figures in the air with the tip of one finger.

Around his neck was an amulet fashioned from a dodo's skull.

Mittle-Mittle watched from a distance.

For the first time in his life, he sensed fear. It was not so much a fear of the wise man, as a fear of something he didn't understand. Why would the people of the land in which he lived keep an old rusty nail in a box, and protect it from one generation to the next?

Very slowly, with sure footsteps over moss, the boy approached the wise man. As he drew nearer, Mittle-Mittle could feel the heat of the flames on his face.

'Excuse me,' he said when he was close.

The wise man froze. He opened an eye. Then the other.

'And who are you?' he asked.

'I am Mittle-Mittle.'

'And what do you want?'

'I want to know why the people of our kingdom keep an old rusty nail in a box, guarding it day and night, and washing the steps to its shrine with tears.'

The boy held up the nail and, as he did so, the old man smiled, his teeth reflecting the firelight.

'Come and sit beside me,' he said, 'and I shall tell you.'

The boy sat down on the soft green moss. As soon as he was comfortable, the wise man began to talk…

The Tale of the Rusty Nail

THERE WAS ONCE a tyrannical emperor in Ethiopia who spent his days counting the sacks of treasure in his many vaults.

They were piled from floor to ceiling in rows of a hundred and one – each of them bursting with rubies and emeralds, diamonds and gold.

Each year, as his wealth doubled once and then again through taxes and foreign wars, the people grew eager for change. Their sons slaughtered in battle, their precious savings confiscated to satisfy their ruler's insatiable greed, they sought a secret way by which to end his run of tyranny.

The problem was that the emperor rarely left his palace, a vast marble structure twenty storeys high, set on the banks of the sprawling River Walaqa, a tributary of the Blue Nile. The kingdom had been plundered to construct the palace, and to fill its magazines with treasure. And, with such poverty surrounding him, the emperor had no interest in ever leaving the luxurious quarters of his home.

So, instead, he reclined in his gardens, or in his grand salons, and allowed his retinue of servants to drop peeled grapes into his mouth, one at a time.

Every so often the secret police caught a group of citizens conspiring against their emperor. The conspirators would be dragged away, hung, drawn and quartered in the main square.

Then their heads were skewered onto spikes as a warning to others.

Now, in this land there lived a small boy, about your age. He had never known his parents because they had been imprisoned in the Slate Tower, which lay on an island in the middle of the River Walaqa. Their crime was daring to question out loud why their emperor required so many sacks of loot when beyond his palace walls there wasn't enough food to eat. So the boy lived with his aunt, a fresh-faced woman with a limp, who was very good to him.

His name was Rintin, and he was the cleverest boy in his school. He never said much, but when he did say something others listened, because what he said tended to be very clever indeed.

One day, Rintin was on his way back from school when he saw his elderly neighbour in chains, being led towards the gallows in the main square. On that day there were so many others in line to be hanged that the neighbour was forced to crouch down and wait his turn.

Nimbly, Rintin hurried over to the old man, greeted him, and said:

'I will save you, I promise, I will save you.'

The wizened old man smiled at seeing the boy, then held up his wrists, weighed down with manacles.

'Keep away from me dear Rintin,' he said softly, 'before they take you too.'

The boy charged off into the back streets, and stopped at the first house he could find. A little girl was playing with her doll outside.

'Tell your parents to go to the palace gates at dusk,' he said. 'The emperor is going to make an announcement. Your parents must spread the word.'

Clutching her doll, the little girl ran into the house.

As for Rintin, he ran on through the streets, warning everyone he passed to gather at the palace at dusk. Once he had reached the end of the town, he made his way to the banks of the river.

With the palace itself so heavily guarded, the only way to observe it unnoticed was from the water.

Borrowing a canoe from a fisherman, he pushed out and paddled his way into the middle, halfway between the palace and the Slate Tower, in which his parents were imprisoned.

Turning his back on the island, Rintin looked carefully at the pleasure dome of the emperor. He scanned the walls, taking in every detail, questioning why it was as it was.

Now, the lad's cleverness derived from the fact that he observed very keenly. Almost nothing ever escaped his attention. He knew, for example, when a storm was approaching because he could sense the trembling of the leaves. And he could tell when his aunt was unhappy because her handkerchief smelled very faintly of salt from her tears.

Rintin's gaze moved over the blocks of marble, looking for gaps, or for an unguarded window amongst the sheering white walls. The stones were flush together, joined in a zigzag edge so that nothing could ever prise them apart.

All afternoon, the boy gazed at the palace.

As the shadows lengthened, he felt a pang of worry, after all the townspeople would be making their way to the gates to hear the announcement. No one would dare stay away, for the emperor was very strict indeed about announcements.

An hour before dusk, Rintin paddled the canoe a little closer to the wall, which was now deep in chill shadow. Approaching, he noticed something strange. Where the walls disappeared at the waterline, there was a knotted mesh of reeds.

The palace was, it seemed, constructed on a kind of giant woven raft, one made from bulrushes. It was incredible that such a mighty structure could sit securely as it did on a foundation so flimsy and feeble.

Scanning the zigzag lines between the blocks of stone, Rintin noticed that there was an unevenness near the waterline. A piece of marble had been wedged into a crack where the zigzag joins were broken, and a definite force was being exerted upon it. But stranger still was the fact that a fragment of wood, no bigger than a matchbox, had been hammered into place beside the sliver of marble.

The wood was held in place with a nail – a bent, brown, rusty nail.

Touching a finger to his chin in contemplation, Rintin made a series of calculations.

By his reckoning, the entire palace was being held by this single nail.

How extraordinary, he thought, that the emperor's mighty seat of power was so precariously in the balance, and all because a craftsman had cut a corner he imagined no one would ever spot.

Paddling his canoe over to the nail, Rintin knocked it up and down with his oar until it was loose. Then, taking a deep breath, he pulled it away from the wood.

Nothing happened.

Not at first, anyway.

A minute passed. And another. The boy cupped a hand to his right ear. He had heard something – a faintest undertone of sound. He gasped, grabbed the oar, and paddled away as fast as he could.

A moment later, there was a deafening noise as the zigzag joins began to part, and the palace began to fall.

Deep in his treasure vaults, the emperor was counting the sacks, ordering them to be rearranged in a new way.

All of a sudden he heard the sound of masonry collapsing in the distance.

'What's that?!' he thundered.

His vizier swiped a hand through the air and oozed reassurance.

'Surely it's nothing, Your Importantness,' he whispered unctuously. 'But I will...'

Before he had time to finish his sentence, the floor of the treasure vault disappeared clean away beneath them.

The vizier, the emperor, and all the precious treasure were plunged into the now choppy waters of the River Walaqa.

Spying their monarch struggling for his life, the guards fled, the palace nothing more than rubble around them. With the sun touching the horizon, the townspeople flocked to the imperial gate.

Rintin clapped his hands and addressed them.

'You are free!' he yelled. 'And never again will you be prisoners!'

He held up the rusty nail, with a bend at one end.

'This nail is a symbol that even the worst despot can be brought down in the simplest way. The great power is power that hangs by a thread.'

The crowd cheered.

Then a wizened old man pushed to the front.

Rintin recognized him as his neighbour, saved from the gallows in the nick of time.

'This boy has saved us,' the man exclaimed, 'and so I vote that we make him our king!'

There were more cheers, and Rintin was carried at shoulder height through the streets. The emperor's launch took him across to the island where he was reunited with his parents.

In due course Rintin was indeed made the king and he ruled for many years.

He married the little girl with the doll, and had six sons, each one wiser and more handsome than the last.

On his desk he kept an orb, and a walnut-coloured box.

And in the box he kept the nail.

After a great many years, King Rintin breathed his last, his beloved queen and many sons clustered around his bed.

The royal family and their kingdom mourned the loss. And, according to his wishes, they buried their monarch in a simple grave on the island where the Slate Tower once stood.

In a letter left to his children, King Rintin decreed that the son with the keenest power of observation should follow him as ruler of the land.

'But how shall we decide which that is?' asked the queen.

The lord chamberlain, who was reading the letter aloud, motioned to the page.

'"The one of you who can glimpse a secret level in a story,' he read, 'will take my orb, my sacred wooden box, and my throne.'"

There was a pause as the sons eyed each other anxiously. The eldest took a step forwards.

'Secret level,' he spluttered. 'Story... *what* story?!'

The lord chamberlain broke the wax seal on a second envelope, and removed several sheets of paper, written in the king's own hand.

'This story,' he said.

The six sons eyed one another again.
'Read it to us,' they all said at once.
And so the lord chamberlain did...

The Shop That Sold Truth

A LIFETIME AGO, in Upper Egypt, there lived a farmer and his wife.

They had very little money, and every month they grew a little more impoverished until, one day, the farmer could stand it no more.

'Tomorrow I am going to the town,' he said, 'where I am going to sell the last of our possessions, so that we can have one good meal before the landlord ousts us from his land.'

'But what will we do after that?' asked his wife.

'We will throw ourselves into the hands of fate,' the farmer replied.

And so the next day, he piled the kitchen table, the chairs, the bedstead and the pots and pans onto the cart, and pulled them himself into the town, a handful of miles away.

By dusk, all the possessions were sold, and the farmer had a pocket jingling with coins.

He was about to go to the market to buy some food to take home, when he noticed a rather grand shop at one corner of the town square. Not having seen it before, he approached it cautiously, and pressed his face up to the window.

The walls inside were lined with tall glass jars. Each one had a label but was quite empty of contents. His curiosity piqued, the farmer dusted himself down and pushed open the door.

The unfilled jars were a little larger than they had appeared from the outside, their labels written neatly in gold script. And it was the labels that caught the farmer's eye. Although he had left school well before his time, he had learned to read, and he read the labels one by one.

'Wisdom, Hope, Perception, Deceit, Truth, Goodwill, Remorse, Bravery, Melancholy...' he frowned and, as he did so, a hunchbacked salesclerk appeared.

'Can I help you, sir?' he enquired in an even tone.

The farmer jumped back.

'I noticed the jars through the window,' he spluttered, 'and was so intrigued that I simply had to come in.'

The clerk dusted a hair from his shoulder.

'And what, may I ask, was it that you found so intriguing?'

The farmer pointed to the empty jars.

'Those,' he said.

The hunchbacked clerk narrowed his eyes.

'And…?' he hissed. 'What is so strange about them?'

'Well, er, how can you sell Wisdom, or Truth… or whatever?' he said. 'The jars are empty. It's as plain as day.'

The clerk, who was growing impatient, cracked his knuckles.

'Whoever said that qualities had a colour or a texture?' he asked angrily.

'But whoever said they could be bought and sold?' the farmer replied.

'Who said they could not?'

The farmer blinked.

'I don't believe it.'

'Why not?'

'Because I fancy you're a trickster, who's set up shop to dupe God-fearing men like me.'

The clerk stepped over to the door and pushed it open.

'It was you who came in here uninvited,' he said calmly.

The farmer was about to stride out, but something caused him to pause.

He slid the tip of his tongue over his upper lip.

'You think I can't afford your wares,' he said. 'Well, I've got money.'

He pulled out a pocket full of coins.

'So what is it you would like to buy?' asked the clerk.

The farmer scanned an eye over the shelves.

'Well, it depends how much they cost,' he said.

'They are all priced differently and sold in small bottles of their own,' the clerk replied. 'The most expensive is Wisdom, and the least is Shyness.'

'Why would anyone want Shyness?' the farmer asked.

'You would be surprised, sir.'

'Well, for a handful of coins, could I get a selection? You know, so I can test some of them out.'

The clerk was about to refuse, when he was overcome with goodwill. He glanced up at the goodwill jar, fearing its stopper was loose.

'Very well,' he said, 'after all, I am about to close for the night.'

Five minutes later, the farmer found himself clutching a sackcloth bag in which were jangling six miniature bottles.

Just before he left the shop, the clerk gave a caution:

'Although they are magical,' he said, 'you have only purchased samples of my wares, and in this size the effect of each bottle lasts only a single day.'

It was dark by the time the farmer returned home. His wife was standing outside the shack and she was weeping.

'We can't go in,' she said. 'The landlord has thrown us out. I hope you made us enough money so that at least we can eat.'

Her husband pulled the sackcloth bag out from behind his back.

'I bought something far better than food,' he said.

His wife looked at him expectantly.

'I bought these little bottles.'

'We need more than liquid, we need *food*.'

'But they don't contain liquid.'

The farmer's eyes were wide.

'Then what's in them?' asked the woman, snatching one and holding it up to the moon.

'It's empty!' she scowled.

'They all are,' the farmer explained. 'And that's the point.'

The next thing the farmer knew, a clenched fist had hit him between the eyes. His wife's fury knew no bounds. As he came to his senses, he thought of something.

Picking up the little bottle that his wife had thrown on the ground, he uncorked it, and held the rim to his pursed lips. He felt something strange enter his mouth, something intangible and warm.

'You've ruined us,' said his wife, as she began to weep again.

The farmer stood up.

'My dear, dear woman,' he replied, 'please forgive me. I can never find the words to apologize enough. You deserve a far better man than I, and so I will take leave of you and return only when I have made something of myself.'

'Good riddance to you!' barked the old woman.

But her husband had already gone.

On the ground where he had been standing was a tiny bottle. Squinting, and holding it to the full moon as she had done before, she read the handwritten label – *Remorse*.

Within a day, the farmer had crossed the fields and reached the edge of the neighbouring town. He met a fisherman beside a stream, approached him and said:

'Hello friend, do forgive me for disturbing you. Oh, how very sorry I am. Truly, I really mean it.'

Struck by the stranger's politeness, the fisherman offered him some grilled fish for lunch. The two men became instant friends and, before he knew it, the farmer was invited to stay in the fisherman's home.

That night, he reflected on the day's events and how the course of his life had changed. His mind wandering, he opened the bag and pulled out the first bottle he could find.

The label read, *Bravery*.

'Hmmm,' thought the farmer to himself. 'I'd like to be brave.' And, without giving it too much thought at all, he prised out the cork and sucked down the bottle's contents.

That night, while the fisherman and his family

slept, a band of thieves broke into the house, each one armed with a scimitar. They came in over the roof, and in through the windows, moving in complete silence.

Then they sprang.

The fisherman and his family were roused from their beds, tied up and relieved of all that they owned.

In the clamour of the attack, no one noticed the farmer sleeping in the kitchen beside the fire. Hearing a commotion, he crept stealthily into the sleeping quarters, armed with a cleaver. And, hardly knowing how he did it, he took the attackers by surprise.

Within less time than it takes to tell, he fought them all at once, and disarmed them all in a feat of unbridled bravery. Minutes later, the band of thieves lay dead, their bodies dismembered on the floor of the fisherman's home.

News of the farmer's bravery spread.

The corpses were taken into the town's main square, where they were hung up for all to see. A passer-by recognized them as the most feared bandits in the realm, with a handsome reward on their heads.

Before he knew it, the farmer was being received in the royal palace, where he was decorated by the king, and rewarded with six bags of gold. Hardly able to believe his luck, he bought an ornate carriage and fine clothes for himself.

Then he set off back to his village to be reunited with his wife.

Unaccustomed to luxury of any kind, the farmer ordered the coach driver to pull up at dusk on the banks of a brook. He selected a spot beneath a sprawling neem tree, protected from the wind by an outcrop of rocks.

'We will camp here for the night,' he said, 'and set off at dawn.'

The moon full above him, the farmer found himself unable to sleep. And, eventually, his mind turned to the little bottles he had left.

Opening his sackcloth bag, he removed the remaining bottles and held them up to the moon for light. But his water bottle had leaked some of its precious fluid and the writing on the labels had been smudged.

As much as he squinted, he was unable to read a word.

'I should open them all and release their

contents into the air,' he thought aloud, 'after all, they could contain harmful elements.'

But something niggled at him and, before he could reason with himself, he had snatched one of the bottles out, pulled away the stopper, and drunk down its contents.

A few minutes passed and the farmer began to sense something. He could hear a distant sound, like the clatter of hooves galloping far away. He looked to the right, then the left, and realized that the sound was coming from the base of the neem tree.

He leant down, cupped a hand to his ear.

A procession of ants was marching across a root, exposed above the surface of the ground. The farmer watched as they made their way across a stretch of barren land beside the brook, and down a hole no wider than his thumb.

The bizarre thing was that he could hear them walking, and talking as well, and he could understand exactly what they said. He could hear the sound of fish, too, swimming through the nearby water, and a nest of magpies up in the highest branches of the tree.

But that was not all.

The farmer walked over to the coachman, who was asleep on the grass. Without quite knowing how, he knew that the man had an eye condition that would very soon make him blind. And he knew that the carriage he drove was stolen, the yellow lacquer having been painted over the red livery of the king.

With his heightened perception, the farmer felt truly alive, for the first time. He thought of all the possibilities, all the things he could do with such a gift.

But then something caught his attention.

The ants.

He overheard one complaining to another.

'What a nuisance it is that we have to dig this mine shaft,' said the first.

'And that there are these great big yellow blocks of metal hindering our way,' said the other.

'If only someone would move them for us,' the first replied.

Wasting no time, the farmer started digging.

Within an hour he had unearthed forty bars of gold, the pure metal glinting in the moon's light.

'I'm rich!' he exclaimed. 'Richer than in my wildest dreams!'

The coachman was woken by the farmer's outcry. He sat upright, rubbed his eyes, and screamed.

'I'm blind! I can't see a thing!'

Loading the treasure into the carriage, the farmer helped the old coachman aboard as well. Then, fearing that the people of his own town would recognize him as the impoverished farmer that he was, he rode on and on until he came to the next kingdom.

Once there, he rented a fine mansion for himself, found wealthy new friends, and set himself up as a member of the landed gentry.

As the weeks slipped away, and as his funds were invested, the farmer became the wealthiest man in the land.

Then, one morning, he remembered his wife.

In all the excitement of his new life he had quite forgotten about her or, rather, had suppressed all thought of her because he was having such a good time.

Changing back into less opulent clothing, he set off in a simple cart to find her.

A few days later, he found her in the town near to where their farm had stood. A few feet away from where she was squatting, hand outstretched, was the shop that had sold the farmer the glass bottles so many weeks before.

But the shop was abandoned, all the windows smashed, the door hanging off its hinges.

'Dear wife,' said the farmer, approaching the huddled figure. 'I have returned and, as I promised, I have made something of myself.'

The old woman glanced up, squinted, and slipped back into the shade. She was imagining things again.

'It's me, your husband!' cried the farmer.

Within a week or two, the couple were installed in their mansion. And as the days went by the farmer's wife grew increasingly used to the lavish lifestyle that instant wealth can bring. She spent a fortune on fine dresses for herself, and was soon bossing her husband around as she had always done.

As for himself, the farmer spent more and more of his time in leisure until, one morning, he remembered the three remaining bottles. He asked one of the servants where his old sackcloth bag had been kept. It was brought to him on a golden salver, rose petals sprinkled around the edges.

The farmer opened the bag and removed the bottles. The labels were far too smudged to read.

'Do I dare?' he asked himself.

There was the sound of his wife barking him orders from the salon downstairs. Grimacing, he summoned his courage, opened one of the bottles and quaffed down its contents.

As before, nothing happened at first.

The farmer's wife asked for a purse of gold, so that she might buy herself a jewel-encrusted necklace. Her husband opened his safe and was about to hand over the coins, when he felt a shiver down his spine.

'If I give her this money,' he thought to himself, 'she's going to ask for some more, and then even more, and very soon we'll be broke.'

So he put the money back in the safe and shook his head. His wife protested, but he walked through into another room, where he started thinking.

For the first time in his life, the farmer had clarity of thought, the kind of which he never imagined was possible. He could think of solutions to the most complex problems in science, in everyday life, and the arts.

On a single day – the day on which the *Wisdom* was effective – the farmer came up with solutions to a thousand things.

He worked out how to solve the kingdom's terrible water shortage, and where to mine the abundant deposits of gold. He settled marital disputes and invented new machines, designed a new city from the ground up, and cured the king of the illness that was about to claim his life.

Before he knew it, the kingdom was wealthier than any other, and the farmer was celebrated as a visionary of the rarest kind. Realizing that his people no longer wished him to lead them, the king abdicated, naming the farmer as his successor.

A little time passed, and the new king's initial genius quickly wore thin.

There were lines of people queuing around the palace, all waiting for an audience – for their king to provide a solution to their woes.

The farmer sent agents across the known world to find the shop clerk who had sold him the potions.

But each one came back empty-handed.

In a moment of desperation he reached into the

bag and fished out one of the two last bottles. He had no idea what was in it, but felt sure it would give him the boost he so badly needed.

Unscrewing the stopper, he sucked down the invisible contents, and prepared for what was to come.

An hour passed and the farmer's wife – now the queen – shuffled in. She insisted on an increase in her allowance, and demanded a new crown.

The farmer king smiled tautly. Then, clapping his hands, he ordered the royal guards to take the queen to the tower.

'I have always despised you!' he exclaimed. 'And will now never have to listen to your moaning again!'

As the guards marched the queen away, the farmer king called his household staff to attention.

'I am doing away with you all,' he cried, 'because I know that you have been stealing from me, and are spying on me, and I hate every one of you!'

After that, he sent a message to the neighbouring king declaring war, on the grounds that the next kingdom was using too much air. And then he roamed the streets in his royal carriage, as his soldiers arrested every third man and woman for plotting against him.

A mutiny ensued.

By the end of the night, the farmer king had been overthrown by his people – all because he had drunk the miniature bottle once labelled *Deceit*.

Stripped of his medals and dressed in rags, he was taken to a small cell below the one in which his own wife was still imprisoned. The cell door was slammed, and the key turned in the lock.

The most wretched of all the cells, its walls were masked in dried blood and filth.

'They'll hang you at sunrise,' said the toothless jailer through the bars as he strode off.

The farmer king crouched down, put his head in his hands, and wept.

'That's enough noise!' bawled the jailer from a distance. 'Any more and I'll come in and thrash you!'

Wiping away his tears, the prisoner coaxed himself to be strong. But his pitiful situation was too much to take. The farmer was about to break down in tears again, when he remembered that around his waist was a belt into which the last miniature bottle had been sewn.

Taking a deep breath and squaring his shoulders feebly, he said to himself:

'Well, what could be worse than what's promised to me – a gallows at dawn?'

He unpicked the stitches, opened the bottle, and drank down its contents.

A little time slipped away, and the farmer found himself feeling quite good. In fact, given his circumstances, he felt marvellous, as if there was everything to live for.

Jumping to his feet, he began scoping out plans for the near future, enthused about the little time he had left. The last grains of sand may have been running through the hourglass, but each one gave rise for hope.

Scanning the grimy whitewashed walls of the cell, the farmer noticed something scribbled high up around the room, in the few inches where the walls and ceiling met. He had missed it before, while lying on the floor in a crumpled heap.

Peering up keenly, the farmer king turned pauper found himself reading what looked like a tale...

Frogland

Back in the days when the world was inside out and upside down, and when humans were the slaves to frogs, there lived twin brothers in the land of Cathay.

Tall and handsome, the first was called Glorious, and the second – who was terribly short and odious to the eye – was named Grotesque.

To say there was sibling rivalry between the two would be a grave understatement. From dawn until dusk, Glorious and Grotesque bickered and fought, because Glorious did exactly as he was told, and Grotesque always broke the rules.

Their squabbling began in the crib, continued through childhood, and then into adolescence, when Grotesque's wrongdoing got them both into trouble.

And trouble came in the most severe form when the brothers attracted the attention of the frogs.

There was nothing that frogs disliked more than humans who made a nuisance of themselves. As rulers of the earth, the amphibians believed that Man had but one role to play – serving them.

The frogs lived in vast twisting labyrinths beneath the ground.

They liked it there because it was damp and cool, and because it gave much misery to their human servants, whom they regarded as unclean and downright rude. The frogs had been in charge for so long that neither they nor the people ever considered that things could be the other way around.

Generation after generation, the humans served the frogs, and the frogs amused themselves by tormenting mankind. They liked very much to point to the pale skin of the people, to screw up their faces and to hiss.

And, they liked to empty Frogland's prison – where only humans were kept – and to take the inmates to the underground pool known as the Abyss, where they were thrown in and forced to swim with bound wrists, until they drowned.

So it was that attracting the attention of the frogs was not a good thing.

Not a good thing at all.

Because the frogs never had a kind word to say to anyone who wasn't one of them.

On a damp chill day, Glorious and Grotesque were brought before the Supreme Frog Council, their hands tied with twine, hoods pulled down over their heads.

The Great Frog Leader straightened his crown, licked the air, and croaked:

'I have it on good authority that you horrid humans have caused a disturbance to our brethren.'

'But Your Frogship,' said Glorious, his words muffled by the covering, 'we are twin brothers, of which there is one saintly one – *me* – and one immoral one – *him*. Ask anyone and they will tell you that there is the good and the bad.'

'Silence!' croaked the Great Frog Leader. 'I will speak, and only I!'

Fearing for their lives, the brothers remained silent.

The Great Frog Leader consulted with his Supreme Council and, a moment later, he gave judgment.

'You are to be cast into the Abyss,' he said. 'And

nothing you will say or do can make us change our minds.'

Before they could protest, the twins were being prodded through the dank labyrinth towards the Abyss.

'It's all your fault,' Glorious snapped as they shuffled forwards, 'I've never done anything bad in my life!'

'You're so damned sanctimonious,' retorted his brother, 'what a tedious life you have lived!'

Silenced by the frog commander, the brothers kept shuffling until they reached the Abyss.

The chamber in which it lay was danker and darker than any other, and had luminous lichens and moss covering the sheering stone walls.

Perched at the edge of the deep pool, the Great Frog Leader ordered the brothers to swim for as long as they could.

With that, they were pushed in.

A great deal of splashing followed, in which Glorious did exactly as he was told. He swam up and down, his legs kicking wildly, the hood still covering his head.

Within a few minutes he had drowned.

Grotesque, on the other hand, disobeyed the

orders. He was damned if a frog was going to tell him how to die. And so, taking the deepest breath of his life, he swam down towards the bottom of the pool.

As he swam, the hood floated away, and he found he could see really quite well. The deeper down he went, the more oxygen there was in the water. So much so that, right down on the floor of the pool, he found that he could actually breathe. By rasping his bindings on a jagged rock, he managed to free his hands.

Glancing around, he noticed that there was a narrow cleft in the darkest corner of the pool. Grotesque swam over to it and, after a lot of wriggling, he managed to scrape through. The passage twisted to the left, then the right, doubled back on itself time and again, but Grotesque kept going.

The thought of the frogs waiting up on the surface to cart away his corpse was reason enough not to give up.

Eventually, a long distance from the entrance of the cleft between the rocks, the surviving twin rose to the surface of a shallow pool. Emerging into blinding sunlight, he stepped from the clear water, a little dazed, but thrilled to be alive.

Almost immediately he found himself surrounded by people.

But they were not ordinary people like him. Rather, they had human bodies but the heads of sheep.

'Baa, baa! He has come!' bleated one of the sheep.

'You are right!' chorused the others.

'Baa! At last! After so many centuries, baa!' cried another.

'The scriptures did not lie!'

'He is so handsome!' bleated the first.

Grotesque stepped onto the dry land and took in the congregation of creatures huddling closer. He wondered if he was dreaming. But before he could give it any thought, the sheep-people carried him away.

The next thing he knew, the twin was reclining in an immense alabaster palace, one that had been kept for centuries just for him. Sheep-headed maidens doted on his every whim, feeding him choice morsels from platters of food. And, as they did so, they sang to him – the sacred ballad of the sheep-people.

Unable to believe his sudden reverse in fortunes, Grotesque congratulated himself on surviving, and on having somehow become a deity to the misguided community of sheep-people.

Each day that passed, the maidens brought food more delicious than the day before, and they insisted that he eat more and more. And, each day, the kind of food that was brought was fattier and fattier – so that very soon Grotesque ballooned outwards in size.

When he refused to eat any more, the maidens fluttered their long sheepish lashes at him, giggling until he could resist no more.

Many days passed and Grotesque found he could hardly walk, so heavy had he become. But, as the maidens reminded him, there was no need for him to take to his feet, because they were there to serve him – to fulfil his smallest whim.

Then, early one morning, the maidens came to Grotesque's chamber in a special procession. Some of them were playing lyres, others singing, all of them dancing.

'This is a very special day, O dearest One!' they called in unison.

'Not more food,' the twin spluttered. 'I just can't eat any more!'

'No, no,' said the chief maiden, 'there is nothing to eat. We are going to bathe you instead.'

Leading the twin through into the royal bathroom, they washed him as he had never been washed before. After that, they adorned his body with perfumes, and massaged him with rare oils.

'This is indeed a very special day,' thought Grotesque. 'I do hope there will be many more days like this to come.'

Strumming on their lyres, the morning air warmed by their voices, the maidens led their guest to the hillside beyond the village where the palace lay. Giggling and prancing about, they looked at him suggestively, and giggled all the more.

As he wondered what was to happen next, Grotesque was taken to a great slab of marble, sprinkled with rhododendron flowers, and anointed with oil. Before he could protest, he was tied down and his wrists and ankles were snapped into manacles.

'What's happening?!' yelled the surviving twin. 'What are you doing to me?'

The maidens tittered and laughed, kissed him goodbye, and wandered away, the lyres strumming as they went.

'Come back! Come back!' shouted Grotesque.

But the maidens did not turn.

Sunset came, and with the night came terrible cold.

Manacled and left to survive the elements, Grotesque coaxed himself to do whatever was not expected of him.

'They expect me to collapse and die,' he said to himself. 'Well, I'm damned if that's what I am going to do. I'm going to survive because that's what I do best.'

Just as Grotesque was trying to work out how to free himself, a giant bird swooped down and began pecking at him. It soon became very clear that the bird was used to feeding on the white marble slab – which was a kind of altar.

By twisting this way and that a few inches, Grotesque managed to angle the bird towards his wrists. A couple of pecks from the beak and his left hand became free. Moving fast, swinging his

71

weight around, he freed his other hand, and then his ankles as well.

Rather than cowering on the ground as some might have done, Grotesque grabbed hold of the bird's tail feathers and clung on for his life as the creature soared into the air.

Far below he caught sight of the lines of sheep-headed people going about their daily work, and the palace where he had been fattened up before ending up as a sacrifice.

Despite the added weight of its payload, the bird reached a terrific height and flapped out to sea. Soaring higher and higher until the air grew thin, it crossed a vast expanse of water, and then a desert, with Grotesque holding on all the while.

From time to time, the great bird seemed to glance down, as if it was aware of its human passenger.

Nuzzling into the creature's plumage for warmth, the twin scanned the landscape below, desperately hoping he might be reunited gently with the earth.

All of a sudden he spied a narrow ribbon of water bisecting olive-green fields, in which farmers were toiling. His fingers strained to breaking point, he waited until he was directly above the canal…

…and he let go. And fell…

Down. Down. Down.

Tumbling head over heels, he fell for an eternity, before plunging with full force into the water.

As it happened, a procession was passing through the fields that day, a cortege of priests giving worship to the land. They were plodding in silence along the margin of the waterway, when Grotesque fell from the sky.

Believing him to be a divine being, they hauled him to the riverbank, pulled him out, and garlanded him with flowers.

They called him 'Opee', which meant 'heavenly' in their language. And they carried him to a mountaintop monastery, where the gods were said to have lived since before time began.

Down in the village, the farmers and their families heard about Opee, and they all wanted to see him. But the clergy barred the doors and insisted that the Divine One was tired after his long descent from the clouds.

'But we want to know all about him,' said the people, speaking with one voice.

'How dare you wish to disturb a divine being?' snapped the head priest.

The farmers went off back to their fields, but their minds were on the Divine One.

And the head priest was thinking about him too.

Having spent a little time with the stranger – a man with whom he shared no common language at all – he soon realized that the visitor's appearance was unpleasing to the eye. All warty and fat, Grotesque would surely have put fear into the people.

With time, the head priest came to see that he would have much more use as a myth. After all, he might well have come as a scout for an invading army, or might even have been diseased.

A full week passed.

Then, one night, the farmers turned up at the mountaintop with pitchforks and fiery torches, and ordered the clergy to show them the man who fell from the sky. Fearing that he was about to lose control of the situation, the head priest slipped into the room where Grotesque was sleeping, and he stabbed him cleanly through the heart.

Solemnly, he stepped out from the monastery, and broke the news to the farmers and their families.

'I regret to inform you all that our beloved Opee has expired,' he said.

The farmers beat their chests, as their wives and children howled at the news.

'We want to see his body!' demanded the growing crowd.

The head priest felt a pang of apprehension in his gut. Showing off the blood-drenched body – and such an ugly body – was the last thing he could do.

So he said:

'How dare you expect the body of a god to be exhibited in death to mere mortals? He must be buried in a grand funeral, a devotion to the land in which we live.'

And so it was that Grotesque was given the kind of send-off that was more usually reserved for potentates and kings.

Carved from jade, his coffin was rolled through the streets in a special carriage fashioned from silver and gold. With every step, the community threw flowers down, and pulled out their hair in remorse. Some of the farmers went so far as to

crawl behind the hearse on hands and knees –
each of them chanting a single word over and over:

'Opee! Opee! Opee!'

A master of showmanship, the head priest had
a massive granite mausoleum constructed in the
capital. The religious elite interred Grotesque,
and lit a sacred flame – which was to burn for
eternity.

Day and night a snaking line of ordinary folk
wended its way up to the tomb, with pilgrims
arriving from far and wide – all eager to pay their
respects to the Divine One.

As the days went on, the head priest understood
that more could be made of the mortal who had
descended into their world. He devised a new
faith called 'Opee' around the Divine One's
existence and, very soon, the new splinter religion
had been embraced by much of the known world.

The numbers of converts surged into the
millions and, as the power of the new faith
increased, the head priest sat down to write the
Sacred Book of Opee, a tool by which the myth of
religion could be spread.

Dipping his quill in ink he had prepared himself
from dry acorns, the priest began to write…

The Book of Pure Thoughts

LONG BEFORE THE earth was hard, or before the
seas were wet, there was an immense temple in
which the gods of the universe resided.

Reclining on great golden sofas, they would
dispense wisdom to one another, through the
days and the long nights. And they would act with
purity – a purity of spirit never to be known in the
mortal world, a world that was to come.

In the centre of the temple was a sacred altar, on
which was kept a single volume. Bound in flaming
red cloth, this book had been written before the
Conquest of Nepsis, at a time when good was bad
and bad was good. Along the spine of the volume
were inscribed the words: 'The Book of Pure
Thoughts'. It was by this teaching that the gods
lived, and by which they were in turn to counsel
the rogue legions of mankind.

The Book of Pure Thoughts explained that, one

day, long into the future, one of the gods would descend, and he would be known as 'Opee', the Divine One. Until that day, the earth would be in a state of limbo. And the era before this celestial arrival was to be known as the Time of Solitude.

In this age, there was nothing that we know now – none of the trappings of civilization, and no fragments of the natural world.

The only exception was a fish.

A beautiful, rainbow-coloured fish.

But because there was still no water, the fish floated through the universe, sucking its cheeks in and out. Waiting.

It waited and waited, and waited and waited, for another form of life to join it, or for the seas to be created, so that it might take a swim.

More millennia passed than were ever recorded. And the fish found himself to be very bored by his predicament. He longed for a river, a sea or an ocean to explore, and he sang a song of solitude to the empty space around him.

Each moment that passed, the fish became a little sadder, and a little more forlorn, his song desolate beyond words. And this went on for an eternity, until the Protector of All Things could stand it no longer. Summoning his power, he sent the great rainbow fish a gift.

The gift of imagination.

All of a sudden, the rainbow-coloured fish could conjure exotic dreams. He found that by clearing his mind he could create entire seascapes, populated with other fish and sea creatures, and that he could imagine the smallest details of each one.

As the centuries slipped by, the fish learned to hone and control his imagination, and he became expert at summoning the most amazing things to mind. He no longer needed a world, or friends, or water, and felt quite content by being entertained through the limits of his mind.

One day, although there still were no days, the fish woke up with a start. He was floating in emptiness as he had always done, but something was making him feel warm inside.

A dream.

A dream he had just had.

A dream that he remembered…

The Fish's Dream

THERE WAS A miser in Persia who was so greedy that he never spent any money at all.

He grew all the food he needed on a patch of bare ground behind his ramshackle home, and he wore clothes he found in dustbins. He had no use for a horse because he pulled the cart that he had built with his own callused hands. People thereabouts used to shun him because he smelled so bad, and they would run away when he drew near.

As time went on, the miser became mute or, rather, he didn't speak, because he was so tight-fisted that he regarded talking to others as an extravagance he simply couldn't afford.

The miser would make sculptures out of scraps of wood he collected in a nearby forest, and he would sell them in the market. Feeling pity on him and assuming he was mute, strangers sometimes bought his pieces.

One day the King of Persia was visiting the market in disguise.

Pointing to one of the sculptures, he asked how much it was. The miser acted out a number with his hands.

'I will give you a quarter of that,' said the king.

The miser shook his head, jumped up and down, and chased the customer away.

A few days passed and the king was sitting in his counting house, when he thought of the miser. Interested in why people behaved as they did, he sent his vizier to ask about the miser who made sculptures out of wood.

'He's the meanest man that ever lived,' said one man.

'He would sell his own mother for a penny,' said another.

'He has such greed,' said a third, 'that he would do anything for a purse of gold.'

The vizier's report came back that evening, while the king was seated in his throne room.

'Would do *anything* for a purse of gold?' echoed the monarch. 'Could that really be true?'

Wiping a hand over his mouth in reflection, the king had an idea.

He ordered the vizier to go to the treasure vaults and ask the treasurer for a small bag of gold.

'Bring it here,' he said, 'and bring me the miser as well.'

An hour later, the miser was escorted into the throne room, his eyes wide from being dazzled with opulence for the first time in his life. He pinched himself, wondering whether he was dreaming. But he wasn't, and he knew he wasn't because the king was standing before him, and he was holding a purse filled with golden sovereigns.

'Hello,' said the king graciously.

The miser squinted a smile. He couldn't bring himself to speak, not even for his king.

'Do you recognize me?' asked the monarch.

The miser nodded and the king jingled the purse.

'Can you hear what this is?'

The miser, who was salivating, nodded all the more.

'Well, I will give it to you,' said the king. 'On one condition.'

The miser shrugged his shoulders expectantly.

'On the condition that you can turn from the meanest, to the most generous man in the kingdom.'

The king stepped forward and placed a gold sovereign on the miser's palm.

'Feel it,' he said, 'enjoy the sense of having pure gold on your skin.'

The miser closed his eyes, his short fingers cupped around the coin. He breathed in deeply, perspiration beading on his brow.

'You have one week,' said the king. 'After which time I will myself judge whether the leopard has changed his spots.'

The gold coin was wrested from the miser's grasp, put back in the purse, and returned to the treasure vault. The next thing the miser knew, he was back home in his hovel.

All he could think about was the piece of gold, and the king's offer.

At first he spat at the thought of it – of becoming generous. *Pah*! But then, as the afternoon wore into evening, and into night, the miser felt his toes tingle.

And tingling toes meant only one thing – that he had to do anything and everything to get his hands on the gold.

The next day, long before the sun had risen, the miser set off for the market with his sculptures carved from scraps of wood. Arranging his pieces on the stall, he stepped back and waited.

Very soon a wealthy-looking man approached him and asked the price of the largest of the sculptures.

The miser did as he always did. He acted out a high price, then stuck his nose in the air when the customer attempted to bargain.

But, remembering the gold sovereigns, the miser agreed grudgingly to the customer's price with a taut, angry flick of the head.

Another buyer arrived a little later, and another, and a fourth.

Each one of them was sold the sculptures at a discount.

That night, as the miser was counting and recounting gold sovereigns in his head, there was a knock at his door.

It was his neighbour, asking to borrow a quilt.

The miser screwed up his face and slammed the door shut. Then, remembering the gold coin, he unbolted the door, and called out through gritted teeth:

'Neighbour, dear neighbour! Do come back!'

The quilt was handed over and the miser went

to bed vexed at having to be generous. Surprised that the miserly neighbour had agreed to lend him anything at all, the neighbour dropped in the next day with a plan.

'Where's my quilt?' snapped the miser.

'Oh,' the neighbour replied, 'I will get it back to you later in the day. But my guest is using it and he still hasn't woken up.'

The miser gritted his teeth once again. He was about to grunt an obscenity, when the neighbour said:

'Our guests are staying longer than expected. Could we borrow your dining table and chairs?'

Remembering the gold sovereigns, the miser had no choice but to agree.

And then, another neighbour caught wind of the miser's change of heart, and dropped in as well.

'Dear friend,' he said, 'could I borrow your bed because my in-laws have just arrived. You know how it is…'

The miser was again going to snarl, when the thought of the coins dazzled him.

'Take it away,' he winced.

For an entire week, the miser struggled to prove

he was as generous as anyone else. He had lost most of his few possessions, and was the brunt of a hundred local jokes.

After seven days, the king's guard arrived at his home and dragged him to the palace. Finding himself in the throne room once again, the miser dusted himself down and dabbed a kerchief to his brow, hoping to quell the stream of perspiration.

The king arrived.

He was in a foul mood, and had forgotten about the appointment with the miser.

'Who are you?' he growled.

'I am the man who was just a week ago regarded as thrifty,' he said.

The king frowned, scratched a set of manicured nails through his hair, and remembered.

'Ah, yes,' he said. 'The meanest man in all the land.'

The miser held up a finger.

'*Formerly* the meanest,' he corrected, 'but now the most generous man that there is, except for you, Majesty.'

'How can you prove it?' asked the monarch.

'Well, Your Majesty,' he said, 'I sold my sculptures for next to nothing, and lent one neighbour a quilt and my table and chairs, and another borrowed my bed for his mother-in-law. I have actually spoken to people as well, just as I am speaking to you now – surely a reflection of my change of heart.'

The king thought for a moment.

'What can you give *me*?' he asked.

The miser froze.

He was shabby at best, and nothing he owned was even remotely suitable for royalty. Gulping, he fell to his knees, and kissed the monarch's signet ring.

'I give you myself, Your Majesty,' he said.

The ruler considered the situation, then he grinned.

'That is indeed an act of supreme generosity,' he said. 'But how will you know what I plan for you?'

Sensing a pain in his gut, the miser shook his head.

'I would never hope or expect to know,' he replied meekly.

Again, the king smiled.

He clicked his fingers and a salver was borne through the throne room at chest height. Upon it was the purse filled with gold sovereigns.

'You have earned these,' he said. 'But now you are mine, you will be my Court storyteller. Can you tell stories? I hope so for your sake. Fail me and I'll have your tongue cut out!'

Pawing his fingers through the coins, the miser nodded.

'Oh yes, Your Majesty, I can relate the strangest tales ever told.'

'Well, don't dilly-dally,' said the king, 'tell me one now.'

But the miser had already begun…

Scorpion Soup

FOUR WIZENED OLD witches were clustered around their cauldron one night under the stars.

Behind them was a sheering rock cliff face, impenetrable and bleak. And a short distance ahead was a chasm filled with thunderclouds and rain.

One of the hags was stirring the brew with a dead man's hand, the others tossing in ingredients for the spell.

'Blood from a murdered child,' said one.

'Pickled eye of an ostrich,' croaked another.

'Egg of an albino crocodile,' hissed a third.

The hand stirred seven times to the right, then seven to the left.

After a long span of silence, the first witch raised the hand in the air.

'It is ready,' she said. 'But who will be the first to taste?'

Each of the witches jostled forwards. But the one who was stirring thrust the dead man's hand deep into the piping hot brew.

Holding its cupped palm to her mouth, she drank.

No sooner had the potion touched her lips than the witch collapsed.

'She is dead!' cackled one.

'*Hah*!' hooted the next.

But the third fell silent. She jabbed a finger at the ground.

'*L-l-l-l-look*!' she stammered.

The witches peered down at their sister's body.

Its appearance began to change.

The layers of skin were peeling slowly back and vanishing. The blood vessels became visible first, then the muscles, the tendons and the nerves. As each of them fell away, the jawline and the skull were exposed, and a gleaming white skeleton beneath.

Her sisters gasped in both horror and delight.

'She is being reborn,' said one.

'Purity,' said the next.

'And when she is pure she will have pure sight.'

Only when every trace of flesh had disappeared

did the skeleton begin to move. Sitting upright, the torso scratched a hand to its face, and the legs struggled to stand.

As it did so, the three sisters sat motionless, the cauldron's fire giving glow to their rapt expressions.

Very slowly, the witch skeleton stood upright, as if hampered by the loss of muscle and flesh. She examined her arm, the empty eye sockets scanning the lengths of bone from elbow to wrist, before moving on to the hand. Then, glancing around her, she recognized her sisters, who looked both hopeful and timid.

'The potion has worked, my sisters,' said the skeleton witch. 'I am ready to open the door.'

Turning, she strode fitfully to the sheering cliff face and held out her arms.

'Mountain! O mountain,' she cried, 'I command you to open your sacred sanctuary and welcome me in!'

A minute passed. Then another.

And, gradually, a grand doorway was revealed, a portico above it adorned with supernatural symbols. The skeleton witch clapped her hands together three times and the door opened.

Beyond it lay a passage, lit by fiery torches.

The witch stepped forwards across the threshold. As she did so, the door closed shut and the doorway itself disappeared.

Squatting around the cauldron outside, the other witches looked on as their skeleton sister vanished. With their impure sight, they had not seen the doorway, or what lay beyond it.

Inside the mountain, the skeleton witch paced through the low tunnel, the torch flames throwing shadows over her bones. Eventually she arrived at a staircase carved from the granite, the steps covered in a sea of tarantulas.

She descended the stairs, the bones of her feet crushing the spiders as she took the steps one by one.

The stairway ended in a sheering wall of carved lapis lazuli. The witch skeleton clapped her hands together once again and the stone barrier shattered, revealing a gigantic cavern – illuminated by phosphorescent fires.

A boiling stream ran through the middle of the cavern, its waters yellow and sulphurous. Around its edge there were hundreds of large turquoise urns, all of them adorned with Chinese characters, each one brimming with the ingredients for supernatural spells.

And at the centre of the cavern was a golden basin filled with squirming black scorpions. Beside it was a pitcher. Without haste, the skeleton witch filled the pitcher from the stream, and filled the basin, boiling the scorpions alive.

When they had cooked sufficiently, she cupped her bony hands together, and quaffed a few drops of the scorpion soup.

Instantly, the witch's skeleton was overlaid with arteries and veins, with muscles, tissue, and skin. But, rather than being haggard and old as she had so recently been, she was restored to the radiance of her youth. Her skin was pink and fresh, her eyes bright green, her long hair blonde and vibrant.

Examining her delicate features in the soup's oily surface, the witch grinned.

'Now I am ready,' she said.

Moving sleekly through the cavern, she stopped at a stone slab at the east end of the floor. There was dried blood on the sides, as if someone had at one time scrabbled desperately to open it.

Leaning down, the witch blew very softly, and the stone crumbled into dust.

Beneath, in another cavern, was a library – a vast and imposing library – thousands and thousands of books. Each was devoted to the dark arts, each one bound in identical blue morocco leather, all covered in dust.

The witch climbed down a cedar ladder until she reached the parquet floor, and began hunting the volume she had come for.

'What are you searching for?' said a voice.

The witch looked around.

'Who… who's there?'

'I am the library,' the voice replied. 'Tell me the book you wish for, and I will give it to you.'

'A talking library?' hissed the witch.

'But, of course,' said the shelves.

'The spell to travel in time,' said the witch. 'I want it! Give it to me at once!'

A warm wind ripped through the chamber, and when it had gone, an over sized tome was sitting squarely on the central table.

'Page six hundred and nine,' said the voice.

The witch pulled back the cover and thumbed her way through the book.

'Six hundred…' she said aloud, '… and nine.'

Squinting to read the uneven print, she scanned the page.

'This is no spell,' she said gruffly.

'Of course it is,' said the library. 'You must read it to activate its power.'

And so the witch took a deep breath, and read…

The Clockmaker's Bride

THERE WAS A family of Persian clockmakers whose work was patronized by the rich, and whose expertise reached the attention of the sultan himself.

Obsessed with mechanical devices, the ruler ordered for the artisan to be brought before him.

The clockmaker was brought to the rose garden in which the sultan was reclining on a spacious divan.

'I shall make for you a clock with many faces, Your Imperialness,' he said obsequiously. 'I will design it to show the time in every realm, with the hemispheres and the planets as well – each of them revolving around Your Excellency's own shadow.'

The sultan touched a hand to his chin. He liked people grovelling, and so did not speak until he was sure there was no more fawning to come. Then he said:

'I have an entire wing of the palace filled with clocks! I have big clocks and small clocks, clocks fashioned from gold and silver, from ivory and the rarest of wood. I have clocks that chime, and others that play dainty tunes. I have clocks that open up to reveal yet more clocks, and I have clocks that tell the time in ways you yourself have never imagined to be possible!'

The clockmaker glanced at the gravel beneath his feet. He didn't want to say it, but it seemed as though the sultan had enough clocks already. Just as he was about to say something suitably fawning, the sultan beckoned him closer.

Apprehensively, the clockmaker approached the royal divan.

'I do not want a clock,' said the sultan.

'Ah,' intoned the clockmaker.

'No, no,' the sultan said. 'Not a clock... but a *chair*. I want a chair instead.'

The clockmaker frowned.

'Then, I shall find a great carpenter, Your Specialness,' he whispered.

The sultan held up a finger.

'A chair,' he went on, 'that is powered by clockwork, and that can travel through time.'

'Through…'

'*Time*. A chair that can travel through time.'

'But… but… but, Your Magnificence,' squirmed the clockmaker.

The sultan brushed him away with his hand.

'Fail me,' he said with almost no interest, 'and every member of your family shall be hunted out and slain, and their bones boiled down!'

The next thing he knew, the clockmaker was in his workshop with a royal command, and with a problem the size of the sultan's ego itself.

'How will I ever make a clockwork chair that can travel through time?' he asked his assistant. 'I have a single month to complete the task. Disappoint the sultan, and he'll swipe off my head, and that's just the start.'

The clockmaker's assistant sighed.

'The only way to accomplish this feat is to enlist the help of a jinn,' he whispered.

'What nonsense are you uttering?'

'The soul of a jinn,' the assistant explained. 'You will need to trap a jinn and to harness his soul.'

'Whatever for?'

'Well,' said his assistant, 'as everyone knows

full well, jinn can travel through the atmos, from one sphere to the next.'

'A clockwork chair powered by means of a jinn?'

The clockmaker's assistant sniffed.

'Indeed, master.'

'But how would I get my hands on a jinn?'

'With a trap.'

'And how would I trap myself a jinn?'

'With a narwhal's tusk, of course.'

There were many things unknown and misunderstood at the time in which the clockmaker lived. But one of them, thankfully, was not how to trap a jinn using a narwhal's tusk.

An hour or two in the magicians' market, and the clockmaker had all the equipment necessary to catch himself a jinn, and to enslave it to his cause.

Turning on his heel, he set off into the desert, where the jinn liked to spend their nights sprawled out on the cool, empty sands.

In one hand he had a basket of green chillies finely chopped and, in the other, a bowl of camphor. And strapped to his back was a narwhal's tusk, the long, twisting strand of ivory catching the last strains of evening sunlight.

A few miles from town, the clockmaker set up a camp.

He collected a little firewood and dried palm fronds, lit a fire, and threw the camphor onto the flames.

A cloud of pungent smoke billowed out over the desiccated sands, dissipating into the night.

The clockmaker waited, as he had been told to do by the jinn-catching expert in the magicians' bazaar.

He waited and waited, and eventually fell asleep.

Just after dawn, as he made up his mind to return home, he heard a rattling sound.

It grew louder and louder, until it seemed as though each grain of sand for a thousand miles was shaking.

Boom! Boom! Boom!

The clockmaker feared an invading army was marching towards him.

Raising a hand to his brow he scanned the horizon.

Nothing.

But the booming went on, the desert shuddering.

Peering with all his might, the clockmaker spied a dust cloud far away. It was heading towards him.

Again, he scanned the distance, squinting into the blinding light.

Eventually, he saw it. Or, rather, he saw something:

A pair of feet as big as boulders, gunmetal grey and moving one after the next.

Above them were the legs and the body, the arms and the head. Colossal, unyielding, imposing in the most debased of ways.

The clockmaker would have run, but his gut told him to hold fast. Terrified, he waited until the immense figure was looming over him. One more step and he would have been crushed into dust.

The creature, a jinn called Mezmiss, stopped an inch away.

Its shadow fell upon him – freezing and dark, it stank of death and destruction.

'Who dares summon me, Mezmiss, Master of all Jinn?' cried the monster.

The clockmaker stepped back, hoping to escape the fearful shadow. But, as soon as he broke free from the shade, he caught sight of the jinn's features

– and wished he had never seen them at all.

'I am a clockmaker, Your Jinnship,' he said. 'And it was I who called you to meet me in this place.'

The monster grunted.

'And by whose authority did you dare to summon me?'

'On the authority of the ivory king!' the clockmaker stammered, his neck craning back.

'Then where is his sword, thou feeble human?'

Holding up the narwhal's tusk, the clockmaker gritted his teeth and snarled as he had been told to do.

The ground shook as never before as the jinn, Mezmiss, collapsed to his knees. Without wasting a moment, the clockmaker ran forwards and threw the chillies into the monster's eyes. And, as he was floundering in pain, the clockmaker climbed onto the creature's head and dug his thumbs into its nostrils.

'I am your master now!' he declared. 'I and only I!'

Mezmiss lowered his head in subservience.

'So be it,' he uttered reticently. 'What is your wish, O human?'

Climbing down, the clockmaker held the ivory tusk up high.

'My wish is for you to travel to another time, and to take me with you.'

The Master of all Jinn snarled his most diabolical snarl, enraged that the mortal knew of the secret formula to harness a jinn's inner strength.

Reciting an incantation as he burned another block of camphor, the clockmaker wore the monster down, until he was no more than a grey, fleshy lump of pulp.

'So be it,' whimpered the jinn, his menacing tone now gone, 'I will lend you my soul, so long as you promise me to return it.'

The clockmaker made a solemn guarantee and, before he knew it, a hoopoe was singing before him in a cage.

'There it is,' said the jinn, his strength all spent. 'There is my soul.'

Leaving the desert, the clockmaker hastened back to his workshop, where he hung the cage on a hook, and got to work. He devised an interlocking gearing system, using hydraulics and dials, astrolabes and cogs, a mechanism that would harness the power of the jinn's soul.

The only thing on the craftsman's mind was preserving his throat.

On the morning of the deadline, the sultan sat perched on his throne, waiting for the clockmaker to arrive, fingertips pressed together in contemplation.

'Perhaps he has fled, Majesty,' said the chief minister.

'Or has taken his own life,' taunted another courtier.

The sultan glanced at his favourite clock as it struck the midday hour.

At that moment, there was the sound of iron wheels moving over wood.

The clockmaker stepped cautiously into the throne room. He was holding a square cage, in which the hoopoe was chirping. Behind him was wheeled a large mechanical device covered in a silky cloth.

The sultan craned forwards, squinting to focus on the bird.

'What is a hoopoe doing here?!' he bellowed.

The clockmaker smiled politely.

'It is more than a mere bird,' he said. 'It is the soul of a jinn, a jinn who can travel back and forwards in time.'

Jerking away the cloth, the clockmaker revealed his creation.

Elaborate in every way, the intricate and interwoven mechanism was encased in glass, so that every moving part could be clearly seen and admired.

At the front, upholstered in crushed vermilion velvet, was a grand fauteuil.

The clockmaker opened a door in the contraption, slotted the bird's cage into position, and bowed deeply.

As he did so, the machine came to life.

The dials began to revolve, the cogs rotate and the astrolabes flash, as they caught light from the crystal chandelier above. In the middle of it all, alarmed by the mechanism around it, the little hoopoe tweeted fitfully.

'It is ready, Your Majesty,' said the clockmaker, a tone of anxiety in his voice, for he had not yet had the time to test his machine.

The sultan got to his feet and stepped over.

'Are you certain that it works?'

The clockmaker looked at him hard, their eyes locked onto each other.

'Indeed, Your Majesty,' he said.

The sultan twisted the royal signet ring on his left hand round a full turn.

'Then go back to the tenth year in the reign of the Caliph Harun ar-Rachid, to the great citadel of Baghdad, and bring me the imperial ring.'

The clockmaker took a step backwards.

He touched a finger to his Adam's apple, at the point where he imagined the executioner's axe would fall.

'A great challenge, Your Majesty,' he said coldly.

The sultan smiled at the corner of his mouth.

'Off you go, then,' he said.

With a deep sigh, the clockmaker stepped up into the chair, the hoopoe still tweeting against the sound of the mechanism. Adjusting the dials, he checked the pressure on a pair of gauges, and pressed a button in the middle of the instrument panel.

With the bird chirping in terror, the machine shuddered and spluttered to breaking point.

Then it vanished.

The sultan's eyes widened; he was too shocked to speak.

Where the machine had so recently stood was a patch of slimy blue jelly.

The sultan inspected it from a distance.

'How dare he sully the royal Court,' he said.

Clinging to the velvet seat, the clockmaker's body was displaced across time, reconstituted at the last moment, as it reached the tenth year of Harun ar-Rachid's reign.

The first sound to touch his ears was the little hoopoe.

He smiled.

'Thank God it is still alive,' he said.

The clockmaker was about to step out of the chair when a party of imperial soldiers marched up, grabbed him, and trussed him in chains. As for the machine, it was loaded onto a cart and taken away, the hoopoe chirping wildly in fright.

As the city of Baghdad slept below, the prisoner was taken to a tower in the citadel complex, with a view out over the Tigris. Beaten and bruised, he was hung up on a cell's wall, a bucket of animal blood hurled over him for good measure.

The jailer, who doubled as a torturer and sometimes executioner as well, held up a pair of pliers and grinned a toothless grin. He was a vile and putrid example of manhood, one who derived pleasure from wielding authority.

Preparing himself for the agony of torture, the clockmaker said a prayer to the Master of all Jinn.

As he did so, the jailer stepped forward, his pliers splayed apart and ready for use.

'Open your mouth,' he grunted. 'And we'll get down to work.'

At that moment, there was the sound of leather boots rasping on stone. An officer from the royal guard had climbed the steps to the tower, and was racing down through the cell block.

Banging on the reinforced iron door, he ordered the jailer to open up.

'Get him down at once!' the officer shouted. 'I have orders to take the prisoner!'

The jailer's face fell. Lowering his trusty tool, he asked:

'And who might have signed these orders?'

'The Caliph Harun ar-Rachid himself!'

The clockmaker was unchained and, the next

thing he knew, he was in the throne room on his knees.

Reclining on a voluminous gilded throne before him was the Caliph Harun of *A Thousand and One Nights*.

A vizier swept through the chamber, whispered in his master's ear, and melted away into the shadows. Narrowing his eyes, the Caliph remained silent for a long while.

Eventually, in a slow and deliberate voice, he spoke:

'I have come to understand that you were discovered with a mechanical device.'

The Caliph touched the arm of his throne in a signal. A curtain was lowered at the far end of the hall, revealing the clockmaker's chair.

His eyes fixed in terror to the floor, the inventor cocked his head up and down in affirmation. So fearful was he that he dared not look up at the Caliph's hands, to check them for the signet ring.

'Your Excellence,' he babbled, his voice barely audible. 'Yes, I created the machine.'

'And what purpose does it serve?'

The clockmaker said nothing, terrified of being executed on the spot as a sorcerer.

The Caliph, master of the known universe, repeated his question, a strain of displeasure in his voice.

'It… it… it…' started the clockmaker, 'is a contrivance by which the spheres of the cosmos may be breached by the frailties of Man.'

Smoothing down an eyebrow with the tip of his index finger, the Caliph walked over to the machine and inspected it studiously. His attentive gaze took in the dials and the levers, the gauges and the gears.

'And what gives it propulsion?' he asked.

'A little hoopoe, Your Majesty,' said the clockmaker.

'A simple bird?'

The Caliph broke into a smile.

'A bird, Highness,' repeated the clockmaker, 'but not a *simple* bird.'

'And where is it, this bird?'

Getting to his feet, the clockmaker paced softly over to his machine, and leant down to where the cage had been placed. His expression went from one of fear to one of extreme alarm.

'The hoopoe has gone!' he cried.

Unable to witness a demonstration of the

device, the Caliph clapped his hands and the clockmaker was taken away, back to the cells.

As for the machine, it was dragged to the stables and left to rust.

It happened that one of the guards entrusted with the job of hauling the machine to the Caliph's throne room had heard the hoopoe chirping. Taking pity on the little creature, he removed its cage and took the bird home, where he fed it some choice little morsels of meat.

The next morning, the guard's daughter woke before her father and, finding the bird there, she jumped up and down with delight. Eager to pick it up and caress its delicate plumage, she opened the cage door.

Instantly, the hoopoe flew from the cage, out of the open window.

Locked up in the tower, the clockmaker cursed himself for his reverse in fortune, and he damned the person who had taken the soul of Mezmiss, Master of all Jinn. He was certain that any minute now the jailer would be along to wrench out his teeth.

The hoopoe flapped its way over Baghdad, the city of gardens, palaces, and fountains. Unable to believe its luck at being set free at last, and to have been transported to such luxuriant surroundings, the bird flew down to a large garden, and began pecking a lawn there for worms.

By chance, the garden belonged to a royal princess, the daughter of the Caliph himself. Her name was Princess Amina, and she loved nothing more than little hoopoes.

Sitting in the shade of her balcony, she spied the bird foraging about, and she gave the order for her gardener to fetch the creature and to put it in a cage.

Within an hour, the bird had been trapped in an unwieldy butterfly net, and it was in a gilded cage hanging in the princess's bedroom. That night, the hoopoe serenaded its new owner to sleep.

And, as she slept, the princess had the most remarkable dream of her life.

She dreamed that a stranger arrived from another time, and took her on a fabulous machine to a land where rainbow waterfalls cascaded down from the sky. And she dreamed that this stranger was the most talented and kind man in existence, but that he was languishing at that very moment in the most gruesome of cells – lost somewhere in her father's prison.

The next morning, the princess awoke to the sound of the hoopoe singing once again. Her eyes wide with wonder, she sat bolt upright and called for her lady-in-waiting.

'You must hurry to the cells,' she said, 'and search out a foreigner who is being tortured there.'

'But how will I know him, Your Highness?'

The princess thought for a moment.

'Take the hoopoe,' she replied, 'and when he sings, you would have found the prisoner I want to see. Bring them both to me – and waste not a moment!'

Just as the torturer was peering into the clockmaker's mouth once again, there came the dainty sound of a woman's voice at the door of the cell. Grimacing, the jailer slid back the bolts to find the princess's lady-in-waiting, a caged bird in her hand.

No sooner had the hoopoe's tiny eye spotted the clockmaker, than the bird began to sing rapturously.

'That's him!' exclaimed the princess's attendant. 'Release him. Princess Amina is awaiting him this very moment!'

With a sigh the jailer unlocked the chains a second time.

Filthy, bleeding, and reeking of fear, the clockmaker was brought to the princess's private salon. He stood in the doorway, his shoulders hunched low, while the hoopoe's cage was hung near to the window.

It wasn't long before the princess stepped in from the garden.

The clockmaker found himself unable to speak, having never before been in the presence of such beauty. And the princess was silent too, her heart warmed by the gentle sensitivity of the stranger.

'Last night, I had a dream,' she began, explaining why she had called the clockmaker to her chambers.

The couple spent the afternoon together in conversation and laughter. They felt drawn to each other, as if nothing in the world could keep them parted.

Then, suddenly, the clockmaker put a hand to his mouth in fear.

'How will I ever get back to my mechanism?' he asked despondently.

Princess Amina leaned forwards and touched her fingers to his cheek.

'I shall help you,' she said.

But word had swept through the palace that a convict had been taken to the princess's private apartment, news that eventually reached the ears of the Caliph himself.

Enraged that his favourite daughter should be fraternizing with a common prisoner, Harun ar-Rachid ordered for the machine, the hoopoe, the clockmaker, and Princess Amina to be brought before him at once.

Setting eyes on his machine, the clockmaker's heart beat all the faster. The bird, the mechanism and the Caliph's signet ring were all in the same room.

But there were armed guards in every corner.

One wrong move and he would be hacked to the floor.

'If Your Majesty should like a demonstration of the machine,' said the clockmaker, plucking up courage to speak, 'I would happily oblige.'

The Caliph signalled to the guard for the prisoner's chains to be unfastened.

'Try and escape,' he said, 'and you will be cut

down before you can touch a finger to your nose.'

The perspiration beading into droplets on his brow, the clockmaker picked up the hoopoe's cage and fixed it into position.

'With the bird installed,' he said, 'the contrivance is ready to be used, Your Majesty. The administrator sits in the chair like this, and arranges the instruments like so. And then…'

Before he could finish his sentence, the clockmaker, the hoopoe and the machine disappeared – leaving the Caliph, his daughter and the guards in astonished silence.

Anyone with sharp eyes may have noticed that the ring on Harun's finger vanished as well.

A moment after it had done so, there was a loud grinding sound, and the mechanism reappeared in plain sight.

Calmly seated on the velvet-covered chair was the clockmaker. On his finger was the signet ring of Harun ar-Rachid.

In one movement, he reached forwards, took the hand of the princess, and invited her to sit beside him. She did so and, instantly, the machine vanished once again.

Back in his own time, the clockmaker prepared

to present the ring of Caliph Harun to his own sultan, but not before he was wed to the Caliph's favourite daughter.

Then, making his way to the palace for his audience with the sultan, the clockmaker dispatched his last duty.

He opened the door of the birdcage wide, and released the hoopoe as he had promised.

The sultan was at first sceptical that the ring had indeed come from the Caliph's hand. Striding through into his private library, he reached up and removed a golden box from a shelf. It was ornate, the edges carved with figurines, the sides inlaid with the finest mother-of-pearl.

With care, the sultan pressed the side of the ring into the lock.

The box snapped open.

Inside was a papyrus scroll that had not been read since the pen of Majnoon the Sorcerer had touched it a thousand years before.

Removing the brittle document, the sultan unfurled it and held it to the light. But the words were unreadable, the alphabet unfamiliar.

Uncertain quite how he knew to do so, the sultan lifted an interlocking catch inside the box, and a slim drawer clicked open, revealing a lens.

Holding it to his eye, the sultan scanned the text.

The words were miraculously deciphered by the lens...

The Most Foolish of Men

THERE WAS ONCE a king who was loved by all his people.

On the day of his first son's birth, a soothsayer was brought to the royal palace. Bending over the royal crib, he declared that the infant would have a long and contented life, and would be adored by all.

'But,' the soothsayer added before going on his way, 'the prince must never – in any circumstances – ever be bathed.'

'Why not?' asked the king in confusion.

'Because, Your Majesty, he is prophesied to drown.'

Accordingly, throughout his childhood, the royal prince was never bathed, but rather sponged down from time to time. A special department was established in the royal household to make sure that the prince's bath sponge never became too moist. And, when the boy drank liquid, guards watched very closely as the glass touched the royal lips.

The prince was kept away from liquid of any kind.

Never permitted to get close to the water's edge at the river, or onto the beach down at the sea, he was protected in every conceivable way – his guards keeping a vigilant eye over their ward.

He was never shown a stream, a lake, a waterfall, an icicle or snow, never permitted to swim, or even to paddle his toes. And, when it rained, he was hastened inside, for fear that an unexpected inundation might claim his life.

Years went by, and the prince grew up.

Then, on the morning of his father's death, he rose to the throne as king. At last, he thought to himself, I shall be able to take control of my destiny, and learn to swim.

But, somehow sensing his enthusiasm for water, his mother stepped from the shadows and said:

'Dearest son, I caution you to keep away from water. You know the soothsayer's prediction. Will you promise me that you will abide by it?'

'I promise, Mother,' he reluctantly replied.

And so the years slipped away, and the young king had children of his own, and lived into old age. In all this time he had never once experienced the joy that water can bring.

Then, one day, the king found it a little hard to breathe. He called his chamberlain, and the chamberlain called the physician royal. As he examined the monarch's chest, the respected doctor prescribed a treatment. But the treatment did not have a positive effect, and the king became all the more unwell.

Called to the regal bedside in the middle of the night, the physician royal examined the monarch once again.

'What's the matter with me?' snapped the king.

His face fraught with worry, the physician royal replied without thinking:

'The trouble, Your Majesty, is that your lungs are filling with water – and you are drowning.'

Within a day, the king was dead, and his eldest son was crowned king.

Despite the coronation, there was much tearing out of hair, and misery and grief. Shrouds of mourning covered the buildings, as the populace struggled to come to terms with their loss. Their sorrow derived as much from the fact that the eldest son was an imbecile, as it did from the passing of his father – an exemplary and popular king.

However hard he tried, the new ruler couldn't think of a way to relieve the climate of national sorrow. To tell the truth, he couldn't really think of anything much at all. He was so stupid that his own family made jokes about his lack of intelligence when his back was turned, and they called him Nums, which was short for 'Numskull'.

Weeks and months went by, and the people forgot how to smile. After all, with an idiot on the throne, there was nothing at all to smile about.

Then, one morning, the new young king had an idea.

He would create a diversion, a diversion to take everyone's mind off the melancholy – a contest, the winner of which would be presented with fifty bags of gold.

'What form shall the contest take, O Imperial Majesty?' asked the vizier.

The king thought for a long while.

'What do the people – *my* people – love best of all?' he asked.

'They love to be amused, Your Majesty.'

A smile crept over the monarch's lips.

He began to giggle.

'Then amusement they shall have,' he exclaimed.

The next day, a herald crisscrossed the capital, announcing the details of the contest:

'His Majesty the king will himself award fifty bags of gold to the stupidest man in the kingdom,' he cried. 'Anyone imagining themselves to be especially stupid may come to the royal palace tomorrow at dawn!'

All at once the city seemed to erupt in excitement.

Wives pulled their husbands out of teahouses, calling: 'Come on you idiot, you can earn us a fortune!' or 'You're the most foolish man I've ever met, you will surely win!'

Long before the sun had broken over the horizon, a snaking line of hopeful imbeciles wended its way through the streets and up to the palace gates. They included a man so stupid that he barked like a dog, and another who had a fork sticking out of his eye, because he had missed his mouth by mistake.

One by one, they were admitted into the palace, where the vizier and his staff examined them. Each one was permitted a full minute to demonstrate how stupid they were, after which most were kicked unceremoniously out of a side door, back onto the street.

A handful of applicants were ordered to return at dusk.

Among them was a man who had married a broom thinking it was a beautiful woman, and an old crone who had raised a flock of pigeons, who was certain they were her children.

Just as the gates were about to be closed that evening, a young man called Yousef arrived. He was holding a package wrapped up in brown paper and string, and was whistling through his teeth.

'Are you sure that you're very stupid?' asked the guard in a threatening tone.

Yousef gave a salute.

'Of course I am,' he said, 'get out my way, for I am the King of Bukhara!'

'Of course you are,' replied the guard, waving him through.

Somehow, young Yousef was mixed in with

the line of finalists. He took his place on a chair, which he turned upside down before perching upon it. When refreshments were brought round by an orderly, he poured them over his head and croaked like a frog.

Eventually, the king swept into the throne room, ready to judge those who had made it through to the next round.

'Who will be first to amuse me?' he cried out.

The man with the fork in his eye sloped into the throne room. He was followed by a woman who had married a clutch of kittens. After them came a one-legged sailor who hopped in backwards.

'Who's next?' shouted the vizier.

Yousef found himself pushed into the firing line.

'Well,' said the king, bored by it all. 'How stupid are *you*?'

Pulling the brown-paper package out from behind his back, the young man said nothing. Rather, he unwrapped the parcel, revealing a mirror.

Stepping up to the throne, he held the mirror so that it reflected the king's face.

'You had wanted to see the stupidest man in the kingdom,' he said curtly, 'and now you can!'

Silence prevailed for what seemed to be an eternity.

The vizier covered his mouth with a hand and prayed. The serving staff dropped their trays and gasped. The other contestants stumbled out in terror. Even the guards winced, fearful that their monarch would go wild with anger.

But Yousef stood his ground.

The king stared at his visage uneasily in the glass. Then, slowly, he broke into a smile, a smile that developed into a thunderous roar of laughter.

'Give this man fifty bags of gold!' he boomed.

Yousef invested the money wisely and was soon one of the richest men in the land.

When he had amassed more money than even the king, he built a university, and arranged for it to be funded from his savings.

Then, having reached the highest level of society, he dressed in his simplest clothing, left his home, and took to the road as a dervish.

Years passed, and Yousef learned the value of men.

And he came to understand what was important and what was not. But, most important of all, he came to know the most vital fragment of human knowledge – something that is lost or forgotten – something that has the ability to turn lives around, and change the destiny of all men.

One evening, finding himself in a foreign land, he asked a hunter the way to the nearest town.

'If you cross the forest,' said the hunter, 'and then the great river, you should reach the town by dusk.'

And so quickening his step, Yousef made a beeline for the forest.

The path on which he was walking wove in and out between the trees, forking once and then again. At the second fork, with the sunlight almost gone, Yousef looked for a place to sleep. He was about to lie on the ground, when he noticed a huge oak tree standing proud in a clearing. There was something about it, something almost magical.

Without knowing quite why, he walked over to the tree and lay down beneath it.

Very soon Yousef fell into a deep, childlike sleep, his body exhausted after many hours of walking.

And as he slept, he heard a voice.

It was calling to him:

'Wake up, O weary traveller,' it said, 'because I have something to tell you.'

'Who are you?' Yousef asked, unsure whether he was still dreaming.

'I am the oak tree under which you take shelter.'

'And what do you have to tell me?'

There was a pause, then the voice said:

'I want to tell you the story of how I came to be rooted here in sunshine and in rain…'

The Man Whose Arms
Grew Branches

MANY LIFETIMES AGO, the tree began, I was a child, a human child in my native Iceland.

I used to run through the fields and the forests, and play with my brothers and sisters in the long summer days. The world was perfect then, and we used to be thankful for the warmth on our faces, and for the soft ground beneath our feet.

But most of all, we were thankful for the trees.

We would climb them, carve our names on their trunks, swing from them, and lie in their branches, talking of all the adventures we would have in the years ahead.

One summer evening, I climbed to the very top of a soaring beech tree, and looked out over the forest. The view was astonishing – a carpet of green, an immensity that could never be dominated, even by Man.

Or so I thought.

Years passed and, before I knew it, I was no longer a child – but an adult with a wife and children of my own. However hard I worked in the town I never had enough money to make ends meet. My wife used to scold me, declaring that I didn't strive hard enough in the market. My problem was that there just wasn't enough work.

Then, one day, I overheard a wealthy man telling a stallkeeper that he had made a fortune in the timber business. He had got the right to chop down trees in a land to the west of our own. My ears pricked up, because the thought of being in the countryside, and gaining real wealth, was extremely interesting.

The next thing I knew, I had become a woodcutter.

I bought the very best axe I could afford, and chopped down trees from morning until night. I was strong and athletic, and found that I could do the job far better than anyone else.

Within a few months, I had paid my debts and had cleared a huge swathe of forest. And, within a couple of years, I was rich, and my wife was dressed in fine satins and silks.

But, as is the way of women, she wanted more. And more, and more.

So, I kept chopping, cutting down all the trees I found in my path – great big trees and tiny saplings. Nothing escaped my blade.

One morning, as I was unsheathing my axe deep in the forest where I was camping, a little turquoise bird flew down and perched on my shoulder.

'Please stop chopping down our forest,' said the bird in my ear. 'All the birds and the other animals are suffering because of you. If you don't stop, the forest will take revenge.'

Swishing the little creature away, I got down to my work and, that day alone, I hacked down thirty trees.

Time slipped by and I made more and more money – so much so that I hired a team of woodcutters and got them to work for me. We bought better and better axes and, each week, I became more wealthy. But, needless to say, my wife found ways to spend all the money I earned.

Then, one morning, I woke up with a pain in my hand. I assumed it was from years of chopping wood, and so I rested.

A few days passed, and a pain began bothering my other hand. A week on, and something very strange indeed happened.

A little shoot began to sprout from my elbow.

Naturally, I was very alarmed. I showed it to my wife. Screaming, she sent me to a doctor, and left to visit her mother in the neighbouring town.

The doctor prescribed a tonic, and told me to get rest. So I took to my bed for a week, drinking the tonic morning and night.

As I lay there under the blanket, the shoot began to grow.

It grew and it grew, and it grew and it grew, until it was more of a branch than a simple shoot. And, at the same time, another shoot sprouted on my other elbow, and on both my hands. Before I knew it, there were shoots peeping out from each finger, and from my ears as well.

I was terrified and ashamed.

No one else I knew had foliage growing from their body. After three weeks, my wife came back from her mother's home. By this time, my entire frame was covered in greenery. Vines were growing out of my nostrils and my face was rough and grey like the trunk of a tree.

And that is what I was becoming – an oak tree.

My wife ordered me to leave the house at once. She said I was bewitched and that I had brought dishonour to our home. Confused and humiliated, I set off, to get away from people. Whenever anyone saw me, they taunted me, calling me an oddity and a freak.

And then, one day, I reached the forest where we now find ourselves.

By that time I had lost the use of my arms, with branches in their place. My torso was more like a tree's trunk than a human body and, with each moment, I felt my legs stiffen a little more. As for my toes, they had become roots, roots searching for soft ground in which to plant themselves. I knew deep down in my sap why this change in circumstances had come.

It was retribution from the forest for having felled so many fine trees with my axe.

The oak tree paused for a moment as a light breeze rippled through its leaves.

He seemed to sigh.

All this happened centuries ago, he said. And I suppose I should be thankful because I have outlived all the people I have ever known.

The tree sighed again.

I wish I could do something – anything – he said, to teach other humans to change the path of their ways.

Yousef, who had listened to the tree's story, touched a hand to the oak's great trunk.

'I have come to know the secret of humanity,' he said, 'and I am devoting what time I have left to making this knowledge available to all men.'

The oak tree rustled with interest.

'Would you tell me the secret?' he asked.

And so Yousef explained all he had come to understand.

When he was finished, the oak tree was overcome.

'I wish I had grasped such a simple and important lesson when I was still a human,' he replied.

The next morning, Yousef thanked the tree for his shelter, and the tree lowered a twig for him to shake.

Just as he turned to go, the tree made the sound like the clearing of his throat.

'I have been thinking,' he said humbly, 'and I want to help you.'

Yousef frowned.

'What do you mean?' he said. 'I don't want to sound rude, but you are a tree. How could you help me with my cause?'

The tree said:

'Last night you explained to me your quest, and for it you will have to spread the word to men. This secret needs to be passed on, and on.'

Yousef nodded.

'But how can you help me, dear tree?'

The oak seemed to stand a little taller and prouder than before.

'From my branches you can make paper,' he said, 'and from my twigs you can fashion a nib. From the oak apples in my high branches you can make ink. And,' he said, his voice quivering slightly, 'when you are done creating a book from me, you can make a beautiful box from my trunk in which to keep that book.'

Yousef took in the mighty oak's wide trunk, its branches, its twigs, leaves and shoots.

'Dear oak, I could not betray your kindness,' he said.

The oak replied:

'Even after I have betrayed the forest, among which I have now lived for an eternity. Cut me down, and I shall begin life in a new form.'

And so, a tear in his eye, Yousef cut down the tree.

He made paper from its twigs, and ink from the oak apples, and sewed the binding with twine. Once he had created a huge tome, standing as tall as a man, he created a magnificent chest to contain it, delicately carved and scented with the fragrance of the forest.

And, on the front of the chest, he inscribed the following words:

My form may have changed once, and then again, but I contain the wisdom of all men.

The chest was then heaved onto a grand cart, and transported to the National Library, where it was given as a gift to all the people of the land.

A few days after the great book arrived at the library, the kingdom was overthrown by an invading army.

Much of the population were slaughtered, including Yousef. All the libraries in the kingdom were destroyed by fire, and anyone found owning a book was burned at the stake.

The invading despot gave the order for the

farmland of the vanquished country to be tilled with salt. So ruthless was his new regime that the people fled to other kingdoms, their lands unfit to be ploughed, their capital destroyed. Eventually, all the people gone, nature reclaimed the ruins of the capital.

Centuries passed.

Where the capital had once stood, a forest grew, giant oaks forming an unbreachable barricade against the outside world.

And then, one day, a hunter strayed into the forest on the trail of a beautiful gazelle, when he became disorientated and lost. Night fell quickly, forcing him to bed down on a rock, itself covered in moss.

Awaking the next morning, the hunter realized that he had been seeking shelter in what appeared to be the ruins of an ancient building.

Surveying the area, he found the enormous carved wooden chest, all covered in creepers and vines. Carefully, he cut away the lianas. And, with all his strength, he pushed back the lid.

Inside, perfectly protected, was a colossal book.

Intrigued at what he had discovered, the hunter forgot about the gazelle, and began to read…

The Hermit

THERE WAS ONCE a hermit who lived in a cave up on the top of a mountain.

Taken there as a child, he was left with a telescope and enough food and water to last him a lifetime. His parents had hoped that the boy would reach spiritual salvation, and would radiate good karma to the universe.

From his vantage point, the hermit could watch the kingdom below, taking in the trials and tribulations of daily life as seen through the telescope's lens.

For days and weeks, and months and years, he watched.

And he watched and he watched and, as the decades passed, the older and wiser he became.

Reaching old age, he sat back and considered what he had learned through a lifetime of seclusion, and of watching.

He came to the conclusion that humans confused the content with the container.

They would gorge themselves on great plates of inferior food, imagining it to be delicious because there was simply so much of it.

Or, they would make halfwits their leaders, merely because they were pleasing to the eye, or because their words were spoken in honeyed voices.

And, when it came to information, they would champion weighty tomes that contained almost no real content, while shunning small books that imparted real truth.

'What can I do to explain this situation?' the hermit asked out loud one morning, as he sat by the cave entrance with his telescope. He was about to go and lie down in the cool shade, when a dragonfly flew into the cave.

With wings buzzing fast, it said:

'Why don't you explain the situation to the people in a way that they can understand?'

The dragonfly flew out of the cave, and the hermit sat there, teasing a hand through his long, white beard.

'I will make a book,' he said to himself, 'a book

that the people down there will appreciate. It will explain clearly how to discern between the container and what is contained.'

And so that is exactly what he did.

The hermit created a book of extraordinary size, using the finest materials, and colours that he knew would attract the attentions of every man alive.

It was kept in a special box, all covered in fragments of mother-of-pearl.

When it was finished, the hermit wrote a message telling the people of the town to come up the cliff face and meet him in his cave.

He tied the message to a stone, and threw it down the mountain.

But, being wizened with age, the hermit was not very strong. The stone didn't make it all the way down as he had hoped. Rather, it became lodged in the cleft of a tree, where it was protected from the elements.

Decades passed and then, one day, a theologian was out walking when he spotted the stone in the cleft, and found the message. Calling for his disciples to walk up the mountain with him, he declared that the message had been sent to him by God.

By this time the hermit had been dead for some years, his body remarkably well preserved by the exceedingly dry climate.

Scrambling up the hillside, the theologian and his disciples reached the cave where the hermit had lived. They found his body curiously uncorrupted, and they found the telescope and the box that contained the book.

'This is the refuge of a saint,' said the theologian, 'and from hence forward it will be a place of pilgrimage.'

Word spread.

And, within days, pilgrims began to turn up.

Some of them sought to be healed, others craved answers to certain situations in their lives.

More still were seeking attention.

And yet more made the journey to the refuge so that they could boast to their friends that they had been there.

One at a time, they would troop into the hermit's bedroom, and would pray over the special box, all covered in fragments of mother-of-pearl.

No one ever thought to open the box.

After all, they regarded it as a sacred relic of some kind.

For centuries, devotees came and they prayed. Most believed that the pilgrimage had cured them, and they told their friends, who hastened to the mountain. A handful were sceptical. But the mass of public belief was so strong that they were ridiculed and shamed.

With time, a monastery was constructed there, and a hierarchy of priests was installed. The pilgrims led to a lucrative business, and all manner of trinket sellers and others set up stalls.

Then, after a very long time, the hermit's box fell to pieces, the result of so many lips and so many hands touching it.

The priesthood wondered what to do. And, as they were wondering, a boy said out loud:

'There's a book inside the box. Why don't you read it?'

'Read it?!' exclaimed the priests. 'How dare you suggest such a thing! No one opens the sacred book! To do so would be to perform an act of unthinkable blasphemy!'

That night, when the priests were sleeping in their grand monastery a stone's throw from the hermit's cave, the boy pulled back the great book's cover, and turned to the first page.

On it was written a single line. It read:

When Man can discern between Content and Container, he will be wise.

The boy turned to the next page... and the next... and the next...

But they were all blank.

Taking this fragment of wisdom, the boy left the mountain.

With time, he became a man, and he developed a celebrated business empire. Those who knew him, or knew of him, regarded him as a leader of men. When asked why he was so successful, he would reply simply that it was because he could discern between that which contained and that which was contained. People thought he was either joking when he said this, or that he was making fun of them.

But almost no one ever paid attention to what he had actually said.

On the last day of his life, the man was walking home when a random stranger stopped him in the street.

'I have something for you,' he said.

'Do I know you?' asked the man.

'No, you don't – but I know you.'

Without another word, the stranger gave the man an envelope.

Inside it was this story…

Cat, Mouse

THERE WAS ONCE an island on which the cats reigned supreme.

They lived like royalty, gorging themselves on the abundant mouse populace, forcing the mice to work for them as slaves.

In the factories and in the mines, the mice laboured from before dawn to well after dusk. All the while, their cat masters became increasingly cruel, and lazier and lazier, as the mice served them.

From time to time a lone mouse would escape his shackles, jump up, and taunt the cats.

But such breakouts always ended the same way.

The offending mouse would be caught, tortured, and slowly devoured while still alive.

Rather than become disheartened at their fate, the mice became increasingly tolerant. As the months and years dragged on, the mice slaves found that they could endure worse and worse conditions. And, as they did so, their feline masters became progressively neglectful.

Eventually, the day came when all the cats fell asleep during the long, hot summer afternoon. Seizing the moment, the mice in the slave camp managed to unfasten their chains, and broke free.

Having tied up the cat guards, they stormed the pleasure domes in which their feline masters reclined. Strengthened by years of servitude, the mice quickly gained the upper hand.

The cats had no choice but to become the slaves of the mice.

Begrudgingly, they did so. But, so hardened by their own experience as slaves, the mice were themselves ruthless masters. Regarding the cats as vermin, they thought nothing of executing them summarily for even the most trifling misdemeanour.

The cat numbers fell dramatically.

Indeed, such was the mouse rage that the cats were almost entirely wiped out. Their numbers reduced to a handful, the survivors plucked up courage and broke free. Making their way by night to the beach, the last cats built a raft with a flimsy mast and sail, and they took to the sea.

Within a day or two all but one had expired.

A scrawny tabby cat, he survived because his treatment as a slave to the mice had been especially harsh. And, as a result, he had learned to harness reserves of strength that other cats never knew they possessed.

After days and nights on the waves, this last bedraggled cat reached another island – an island ruled over by ghouls.

Fearsome in looks and demeanour, the ghouls had a legend that one day a saviour unlike them would come from the distant horizon, and would rule over them. Every ghoul child was raised with the legend and could quote it by heart.

Each morning and night, all the ghouls clustered together on the sands to peer out to where the water met the sky.

Centuries had passed, and no saviour ever came.

But still they waited.

And they never gave up hope.

Searching the horizon for their saviour became important in itself – a kind of divine act by which the ghouls lived. Gathering together twice a day as a community kept the society strong, and was a way by which traditions and folklore were passed from one ghoul generation to the next.

On the evening of the cat's arrival at the island, the ghouls were clustered down at the beach, singing a song venerating their saviour – the saviour who had never come. Some of them had forgotten why exactly they met there twice daily. Yet in many ways it didn't seem to matter why they were there, so much as the fact that they were.

'Look there!' cried one of the ghoul children suddenly, pointing to the distance.

'Keep singing and stop making a noise,' snapped one of the ghoul elders.

'Father, look!' exclaimed another of the children.

A surge of anticipation swept through the group, as all the ghouls – young and old – set eyes on the raft.

The cat was pulled to safety, and was taken at once to the house that had been built for the saviour, were he ever to come. Fed delicious morsels of fish, he was fanned with palm fronds, and told over and over how very special he was.

Unable to believe his luck, the cat enjoyed the

indulgence for a long while. He learned to speak the ghoul language, and became well-versed in the ghoulish lore and traditions, of which he himself was part.

But, now that their saviour had arrived, the ghouls' society began to collapse. With no reason to cluster down at the beach, the ghoul community became fragmented.

The legends and the songs were forgotten.

And then, eventually, the ghouls began to question why they had to support such a lazy tabby cat, even though he was supposedly their saviour.

Fortunately, one of the ghouls was more enlightened than the others, and realized what was happening. Little did he know that it was his ancestor who had devised the idea of the ghoul saviour arriving, as a device to keep the community in harmony.

After much consideration, he poisoned the cat as he slept.

Beside the now bloated feline body, he left a document.

When they found the remains of their saviour, the ghouls were disconsolate. They jumped up and down, and beat themselves with sticks.

'What will we do now that our saviour has left us?' they cried as one.

The enlightened ghoul jabbed a hand towards the document.

'The saviour may have gone to new hunting grounds,' he said, 'but he has left us this. It will become the core of our new faith,' he said, 'and will be repeated day and night by us all down on the beach.'

The ghouls hurried down to the sands.

'We want to hear it, and we want to worship our saviour, the cat,' they called.

When they were all clustered together before the setting sun, the enlightened ghoul read the story to the others, as they listened…

The Singing Serpents

ONCE UPON A time there lived in Arabia a wise cat.

This wise cat always had enough to eat and drink, and was pampered by his human masters. But he dreamed of something else. He dreamed of something magical to inspire him, something to warm his heart.

The other cats thought he was senseless. They told him to remain quiet, to live his life as they all did, being looked after by Man.

'We have existed like this for thousands of years,' they told him, 'and we are very good at it. We have the lifestyle perfected, a lifestyle in which humans give us plenty of food and attention, and we need to provide almost nothing in return.'

But the wise cat didn't listen to them.

He knew that the only thing that mattered in life was to make his own path – a path that the foolish cats didn't realize existed at all.

And so, the wise cat packed a knapsack, and set off in search of his destiny.

Within minutes of his departure, all the other cats had forgotten about him. They went back to their chunks of juicy meat, to their big bowls of milk, and to the attentions of mankind.

The wise cat travelled from one kingdom to the next, learning languages and immersing himself in different lands. And, with each day that passed, the wise cat became all the wiser.

Now, one day, the cat reached a country ruled by dogs. There were big gruff dogs, little yapping dogs, dogs that were kind to cats, and others that were not. With no other cats there at all, the wise cat had no choice but to spend his time with the dogs. He found them to be quite easygoing, and less complicated than his own species.

Dogs, as he reasoned it, were all bark and no bite.

There was nothing that got the dogs worked up, nothing except the subject of singing snakes. The mere mention of the reptiles threw every dog in the kingdom into a wild frenzy of fear and reaction.

'Singing snakes come in the night and swallow you whole,' one of the dogs told him.

'They have teeth like knitting needles,' another revealed.

'They hypnotize you with their eyes, and there's nothing you can do to break free!' exclaimed a third.

The wise cat listened to the dogs and said nothing.

When they were finished, he asked:

'Have any of you dogs ever seen a singing snake?'

The dogs shielded their eyes with their paws in terror.

'No, no, of course not,' they howled.

'So, how do you know that you are really afraid of singing snakes?' asked the cat.

Standing on his hind legs, the smallest dog, a Pomeranian, said:

'Because we all know that we are, and that's that!'

A few weeks passed, and the wise cat lived quietly among the dogs. He was always polite, and the majority of the dogs treated him well. From time to time he was chased. But, mostly, the dogs left him alone. Instead of disliking him, they regarded him as something of a novelty.

Then, one night, an elderly dog had a dream.

Or rather, it was a nightmare.

He dreamed that a plague of singing serpents was about to strike – a race of evil reptiles dead set on swallowing all the dogs whole.

Word of his dream spread like wildfire and, as it did so, the entire community was thrown into disarray.

'What are we going to do?' yelped the dogs. 'We are powerless. The singing snakes will swallow us whole!'

Sitting on a fence in the middle of the town, the wise cat listened to the fuss. And he watched as the normally level-headed dogs worked themselves into a frenzy about an old dog's ludicrous dream.

By the afternoon, the dogs were digging holes on a large scale – holes to hide in when the singing-snake invasion took place. After that, they convened an emergency council in their great hall, to which all dogs were invited to debate the worrying state of affairs.

As he was the only cat in the kingdom, the wise cat was allowed to come along. He listened to the many speeches, all of them tinged with hysteria and fear. And he watched as the canine community grew ever more agitated.

By the end of the evening, he could stand it no more.

He jumped up onto the podium.

'I may be just a cat,' he said. 'But that gives me an advantage.'

The dogs looked confused.

'What is it – your advantage?' they barked.

'It is that I can see your situation from the outside, while you can only see it from within.'

'So what?' snapped the dogs.

'Well, it means that I can see how to solve your problem.'

A few dogs at the front of the hall began barking ferociously.

'Tell the cat to get out!' they growled. 'This is dog business!'

But the old dog that had had the dream in the first place called for hush.

'Let the cat speak,' he snarled.

And so the wise cat continued:

'Because I am not one of you, I have been able to watch you with detachment,' he said. 'And I

have seen that you dogs are easygoing. But...'
the cat paused to take in his audience, 'the idea
of singing serpents has thrown your lives upside
down. Why is that?'

'Because serpents swallow dogs whole!' barked
a Chihuahua anxiously at the back. 'And every
dog alive knows that!'

'Let me ask a question,' replied the wise
cat. 'How many of you have ever seen a singing
serpent?'

There was silence. Then, a Labrador pointed
at the old dog.

'He has,' he yelped. 'Old dog has seen one, in
his dream!'

The wise cat smiled demurely.

'In his dream,' he said.

A wave of murmuring swept through the room.
The dogs didn't like the idea of a cat – however
wise – trying to make fun of them. But mockery
was not on the cat's mind.

Rather, he raised a paw very slowly, and said:

'My dear dog friends, good fortune smiles on
your community. You see, as chance would have
it, I was sold something in the next kingdom,
something very precious and very powerful...

something that can protect us all from the singing snakes.'

'What is it?' barked the dogs anxiously.

The wise cat held something above his head.

Something very small and shiny.

Craning forwards, the dogs were eager to know what it was. They clambered over each other, eyes wide, mouths drooling, noses sniffing.

'This is an amulet of awe-inspiring power!' exclaimed the wise cat. 'It was made by a famous magician to protect its owner from the danger of singing serpents!'

The dogs gasped. They yelped. Some howled. All were relieved.

'You have all been good to me,' the wise cat said, 'and so I am presenting the amulet to you all as a gift – a gift of my affection!'

'We will make a special shrine for it!' yelped a spaniel.

'We'll guard it and look after it!' growled another dog.

'We will devote our lives to it!' barked a third.

The cat seemed pleased.

Jumping down from the podium, he passed the sacred amulet to the old dog.

'Make sure you protect it,' he said. Then he left.

Clustering around, each of the dogs gave thanks to the wise cat for saving them from the invasion of the singing snakes – an invasion that was thwarted at the last moment...

By an ordinary metal button.

As for the wise cat, he came to realize that his work in the land of the dogs was done.

Slinging his knapsack over his shoulder, he took to the road once again.

Many lands passed beneath his paws.

Some were at peace and others were at war. More still were in a mixture of the two, or were realms in which mediocrity reigned.

The wise cat roamed on and on, and judged no one and no thing.

Then, one night, he was at a bleak caravanserai beneath the glinting stars, when he overheard a story being told.

So strange was it, that the tale filled him with wonder and with horror in equal measure.

Within an hour of hearing it, the wise cat was paralyzed. He was unable to move. The only thing he could do was to hum.

None of the other listeners that night was affected in the least by the story. Indeed, they all fell straight to sleep and, next morning, forgot they had heard a tale at all.

But then, stories have a way of working in different ways, depending on who is receiving them.

His body stiff like wood, the wise cat managed to communicate with the young daughter of the man who owned the caravanserai, by humming. They made a language from a range of humming sounds, a language all of their own.

Over months the little girl and the wise cat developed a friendship, the most remarkable friendship of either of their lives. It was a friendship that would not have come about had the wise cat not heard the story, and been paralyzed as a result.

Through many weeks and months, the wise cat hummed to the girl.

And, through the hums, he recounted a tale...

The Princess of Zilzilam

THERE WAS ONCE a green jinn who, tricked by a magician, had lain trapped inside an ugly lead urn for a thousand years and a day.

As he languished there, the jinn vowed that he would wreak havoc on mankind if he were ever to get free.

He waited. And he waited.

And he vowed and he vowed.

But the urn in which the jinn was imprisoned had been thrown by the magician into the deepest stretch of the Red Sea.

And there it lay for an eternity.

Until, one dark night, it was moved by a rogue current, and then swept up in a fisherman's net as it raked across the sea floor.

The net was hauled up onto the deck, and the urn was discovered.

Hopeful of finding treasure, the captain wasted no time in breaking the lead seal.

Within an instant, the green jinn had surged from the container, slain the captain and his men, and drunk all the blood in their veins.

Soaring up and up into the night, his form billowed outwards and upwards, until he became the sky and the heavens.

'I vow to slaughter every living thing on this earth!' he declared. 'And shall not rest until every heart – human or animal – has been extinguished, and until I have devoured every last drop of blood!'

With that, the green jinn opened his mouth and bore down on the city of Alexandria.

Believing that an eclipse was taking place, the people ran into the twisting streets of the old city and gazed up at the sky.

What they saw in its place was more terrifying than any far-fetched nightmare.

The green jinn's mouth was leering down towards them, a kaleidoscope of carnage: fifty rows of blood-stained teeth, the rotting, festering cadavers of unknown dead.

The diseased.

The putrefying stench of death.

Blood, blood, blood.

The people of Alexandria charged about in all directions, fleeing for their lives. Some hid under their beds. Others dived into empty barrels. More still threw themselves into the sea.

Standing in the middle of the main street was a young man called Adam. Unlike the other people panicking around him, he was not fearful of the sight.

Rather, he was intrigued.

A fraction of a second before the jinn's mouth claimed its prey, Adam raised an index finger high above his head, and called out:

'Whatever depraved creature you are, desist for a moment, until you have heard what I have to say! Not to allow me to speak would be an act of despicable cowardice!'

It just so happened that the green jinn was troubled by almost nothing at all. But the thought of being regarded as a coward vexed him greatly.

So he paused, his mouth in mid-attack, his eyes rolling with rage.

'How could you consume us,' shouted Adam as loudly as he was able, 'without informing us why you are doing so?'

The green jinn shook with rage. And, as he shook, the heavens shook, and the world shook as well.

'Your pitiable race entrapped me in an urn for a thousand years and a day!' he roared. 'And you, and all other living things, shall now pay the price of my wrath!'

With the people of the city hastening about in terror around him, Adam touched a fingertip to his chin.

He thought for a moment, then he said:

'Well, O mighty creature, surely you would wish to talk to me before you snuff out my life.'

The jinn drew breath to speak. And, as he did so, the palm trees on the coast were sucked back, as if a storm was about to make landfall.

'I have no time to waste in meeting my victims one by one!' he spat.

But, just before the monster could utter another syllable, Adam held up his finger again.

'I feel embarrassed to tell you this,' he said slowly, 'but everyone is gossiping about you in the lanes of the old city.'

'No doubt they are declaring how fearsome I am!' cried the monster.

'Alas, they are not, O great one,' Adam replied.

The jinn narrowed his eyes, each one the size of the moon.

'I shall slay you first for uttering lies!'

Adam held his ground, his head cocked back as he took in the creature's immense form.

'They are saying that you're attacking us out of fear,' he said, 'and out of sheer cowardice. They say that you couldn't harm an ant let alone a great city such as Alexandria!'

'*Pah!*' exclaimed the green jinn. 'I could swallow the entire city whole! And I will!'

Swelling in size until even larger than before, the monster once again bore down.

But Adam laughed at the sight.

'Your cowardice is surely proven by your size,' he said. 'Any creature so enormous could destroy an entire city. The challenge would be to cause the same harm when smaller in scale.'

The green jinn emitted a crazed shriek of fury. So loud and violent was it, that the ground buckled as though struck by an earthquake.

'I could slay you all if I were half the size!' he boasted, before instantly reducing his form to the size of a mountain.

Adam held up a finger.

'You are still very big,' he said, 'and it is making conversing with you challenging. Could you not make yourself a little smaller?'

The green jinn shrank again, from the size of a mountain, until he was the height of a giant, a giant in human form. His mouth packed with sharp yellow teeth, each one framed in red, he loomed down over Adam.

'Speak your last words O mortal!' he bellowed.

Adam touched a finger to his chin once again.

'Surely even a giant could exact terrible damage on a place like this,' he said. 'But that's not what the people of Alexandria think. As I told you, they say that you couldn't harm an ant!'

The green jinn turned purple with wrath, his mouth dripping with blood.

'Show me an ant, and I shall smite it!' he exclaimed.

Adam leant down, and pretended to pick a speck from the ground.

'Here is an ant,' he said.

Filling his lungs with air, the jinn was about to blow a jet of fire down at the ant, when Adam said:

'As everyone knows, the people of Alexandria are very hard to impress. They take any opportunity to make fun of people from outside the city. And if they see a giant killing an ant – well, that's not going to impress them at all.'

The green jinn released his breath. He frowned.

'Well, what would impress them?' he asked. 'And tell me swiftly, or I shall snuff you out as soon as look at you.'

Adam thought for a moment, and replied:

'Well, surely, what would impress them would be for an ant to be dispatched by something even smaller than it, like a flea.'

The green jinn spat blood.

'I have dignity, you know!' he exclaimed. 'I am a great jinn, and am not going to transform myself into a flea.'

'A pity,' said Adam. 'Then the people will gossip about you all the more.'

'But I am just about to kill every last one of them!' bawled the green jinn. 'So I really don't care what they say!'

Adam sighed.

'But surely as a creature of such dignity and poise, you would feel all the more satisfied were you to prove your strength by such an insignificant act as killing an ant.'

Spitting more blood and then fire, the green jinn reduced his size from that of a giant to that of a flea.

'Show me the ant,' said a faint voice, 'so that I may smite it at once!'

But Adam wasn't listening. Instead, he stepped forwards and ground the sole of his sandal into the dirt, until the green jinn was quite definitely dead.

Word of his bravery and cunning spread through Alexandria, and Adam was hailed as the city's saviour. Gifts and titles were lavished upon him, and the wealthiest members of society sought to marry him to their most beautiful daughters.

But, courteously, Adam refused all the awards, the gifts, and the invitations to wed.

Packing a simple leather satchel, he set out into the desert, hoping to have a little time and space to think.

With the stars glinting in the heavens above, he sat beside his campfire. Staring into the flames, his mind thought about the frailty of jinn and of men.

Suddenly, Adam heard a voice.

'Adam, dear Adam,' it said. 'My name is Leila, and I am the daughter of the King of Zilzilam. I am trapped beneath the very sands on which you are camped. Rescue me and I promise to fill your heart with joy.'

Adam twisted round to the left, then the right. The enveloping darkness was empty of any life.

'I can't see you,' Adam whispered. 'Am I imagining you?'

The voice came again, a little louder than before, running on the breeze.

'I am trapped beneath the sands. Walk ten paces south of the fire. Dig down with your hands, and you will find a stone slab. Pull it back and descend.'

Half-wondering whether he was dreaming, Adam glanced back at the fire. The embers were glowing now, fanned by the wind.

He was about to curl up on his blanket and sleep, but the voice came a third time:

'Please come and save me, dear Adam, I beg you…'

Adam got to his feet, and counted ten paces south of the campfire. Then, kneeling, he dug down through the cool sand with his hands. He was about to give up, when his fingertips touched something hard.

Stone.

Digging faster, he unearthed a granite slab, a great iron ring set squarely in the middle. Without giving it any thought, he yanked the ring with all his strength, and the slab slid easily away.

Adam peered down the hole into a dawn realm.

Squinting, he made out a kind of tropical jungle: a profusion of trees and luxuriant vines, of insects and suffocating heat. Climbing down through the boughs of a colossal tree, he made his way onto the forest floor.

As he stood there, taking in a scene from a dreamscape, the first light broke through.

A pair of suns rose both at once – one in the east, the other in the west.

Shading his eyes, Adam watched as the jungle came to life.

Animals he had never seen before swung from one vine to the next, or prowled between the trees, hunting their morning prey.

There were sloths with two heads, zebra in rainbow stripes, and cheetahs weighed down with mighty ibex horns. And there were giant anteaters, as well, and mice with human-like hands and feet, and spiders the size of antelopes.

Through the jungle wafted the voice once again:

'Clear your mind of everything you know, Adam,' it cautioned, 'and place one foot before the other. Whatever you do, do not glance down at your feet.'

'How do I know that I can trust you?' Adam thought.

Reading his mind, the voice answered:

'You do not, and that's why you can.'

Doing as he was told, Adam trod a path through the trees, taking care not to look down. As he paced along, he smelled the aroma of roasting meat, and the tart scent of bitter oranges. Then he felt a strange sensation… a sensation of something crawling over his feet and legs.

Straining to obey the voice, he forced himself to refrain from looking down. But the smell and the tingling became too great. Unable to withstand a moment more, Adam lowered his gaze.

Horror is too feeble a word to describe his distress.

His feet and legs were sheathed in squirming worms, glowing red as they gnawed at his flesh. And, as they did so, they emitted a coating of waxy oil, a kind of anaesthetic.

Fearfully, Adam swished the worms away.

But as he did so more appeared, until his hands were covered in them as well.

As he fought in a frenzy to rid himself of the scourge, the voice came once again. Soothing and calm, it drifted effortlessly through the trees.

'Rip off your shirt,' it said, 'and allow the worms to feast on your chest.'

'But they're killing me!' Adam shouted out loud.

'Trust me,' said the voice.

Without any other choice, Adam tore off his shirt. The worms slithered all over his chest, glowing red as they got to work on it.

But, quite suddenly, they began to turn purple-blue and fall away as scabs.

Adam tramped on through the suffocation of trees, following the voice.

The undergrowth became increasingly dense, until it was a struggle to make any headway at all.

Progressing inch by inch, Adam began to sense grave danger.

Something deep inside was cautioning him to turn back, to flee. But, as before, the voice soothed him, luring him forwards.

All of a sudden the trees gave way to a wide clearing. The ground there was infested with orange beetles, armed with crab claws.

In the middle of the glade was a primitive machine.

The sides consisted of three pairs of multiple scimitars, each one attached to a flywheel. The central unit was a mass of cogs and levers, with a large pair of scales at the front. But the base of the creation was not mechanical at all.

It was alive.

Avocado-green and scaly, it was the colour and consistency of an alligator's back, and was moving slowly, as if rearranging itself.

Approaching cautiously, crunching a path through the orange beetles, Adam took in the details of the outlandish contraption. As he drew close, he noticed something – something that caused his feet to root themselves in the ground.

A woman was encased in the central unit.

Strapped down, she was unable to move. The scimitars were angled in such a way as to carve her up if she tried to escape. Without being told, Adam knew that the woman was Princess Leila.

'I shall disarm this *thing* and release you!' he exclaimed, quite overcome with sorrow.

The princess did not reply.

Not at first.

She just blinked, the rest of her body held rigid. Then, telepathically, she said:

'Dear Adam, I am indebted for your bravery. But there is only one way to rescue me. In the pans of the scales you will need to place two objects. The first is Hope, and the other – Fear. Attempt to disentangle me, and I shall be chopped to pieces.'

'But Hope and Fear have no form,' Adam said. 'They are invisible, intangible.'

The princess blinked once again.

'It is for you to find them,' she replied, a tear running down her cheek.

'Where shall I search?'

'In your heart.'

Adam reached forwards, until his hand was no more than an inch from the machine. He could feel the princess's warmth.

'I will save you,' he said. 'If I have to scour the universe for Hope and for Fear…'

With that, he was gone.

Retracing his path once again to the surface, Adam found himself at the campfire, the embers still crackling and spitting in the breeze. Leaning back on his haunches, he pondered how and where to find the qualities needed for the scales.

'I shall set out at dawn, and travel the world,' he whispered, 'and will not give up until I have captured Hope and Fear.'

Before the sun had broken over the horizon, Adam's footsteps stretched in a line to eternity.

He walked through days and nights, seeking out anyone who could help him with his quest.

In the next kingdom, he met a hermit who listened to his tale. When he had heard it, the recluse instructed him to search out the Blue Mountains. Because only there, the hermit insisted, could the riddle be solved.

At the Blue Mountains, Adam was informed by a diviner that the only way to find Fear and Hope was not to search for them at all.

Undeterred, he kept searching.

He walked and he walked, and he walked and he walked, until he had crossed half the known world. Each person he asked pointed him in the direction of another, until he was despondent and almost broken. His health suffering from worry, he realized how deeply he had fallen in love with Princess Leila.

After many months of adventure, he found himself in the middle of nowhere – at the desert campfire where his journey had begun.

'I have failed you, dearest Leila,' he said in a whisper, his words carried away on the breeze.

'No, no, you have not, Adam,' came the voice. 'Look into your heart and you will know what to place on the scales.'

Plunging his head in his hands, he struggled to reach a decision.

But he could not.

And so, unable to carry on, he paced over to the stone slab, and descended back into the jungle world in which the King of Zilzilam's daughter was kept prisoner.

Although months and years had passed on the surface, it seemed as if the sands of the hourglass fell far more slowly in the jungle realm than they did above. Hardly a day had gone by since he had embarked on his quest.

Wending his way through the trees, Adam retraced his path towards the glade in which the princess was imprisoned. As he walked fitfully between the vines, he noticed a mango tree, its ripe fruit hanging down in great quantities.

Overcome with hunger, he picked one of the mangoes and ate it.

Within a few feet of the tree, he reached the glade in which the machine was still standing. As before, the scimitars were razor-sharp, glinting in the blinding light.

While he watched, they began to move as if his arrival had triggered them. The scimitars scythed alarmingly through the air and, as they did so, the machine's reptilian underbelly coursed back and forth, surging to life.

'Please hurry!' whispered the princess. 'Precious time is running out. In moments, I fear I shall be dead!'

Adam stood before the machine, his blood fortified with adrenalin. Although desperate to rescue the princess, he felt helpless. With her certain death a moment away, Adam knew he had to try something.

As he conjured up the courage to overcome his fear and destroy the machine, he felt his face and hands running with perspiration.

'Fear,' he thought, wiping his forehead dry. '*This* is Fear!'

Rinsing a hand over his brow once again, he collected a few drops of sweat, and dripped them into the left pan of the scale.

But what about Hope?

Drawing a deep breath, Adam was about to resign himself to failure, when he remembered the mango seed, still clutched in his hand.

'*This* is Hope,' he said. 'The Hope of a mango tree.'

In a quick movement, he dropped the seed into the second pan.

The machine whirred and grunted, the scimitars flashing in the jungle light.

And, all of a sudden, the straps and bindings disintegrated.

Princess Leila was free.

Adam and the princess returned to the surface, and to the Land of Zilzilam.

Forty days of celebration were held, so overjoyed was Leila's father that his favourite daughter had been saved.

When the festivities were at an end, Adam and the princess were married in a tumultuous marriage ceremony.

Another forty days of festivities followed.

And, with time, Adam ascended to the throne of Zilzilam, reigning as its king for many years. His wisdom and courage are still spoken of today, and his acts of kindness are the stuff of legend far beyond the ancient walls of Zilzilam.

As the years passed, King Adam devoted more and more of his time to improving the kingdom, and the living standards of its people. He made sure that everyone had enough food and a good education, and that every citizen had the opportunity to come to him directly with their problems. The gates to the palace were always open, and everyone knew that King Adam would see them if they needed his help.

One evening, when he had ruled for seventeen years, Adam was sitting in the durbar attending to some official papers. As he pressed his signet ring into a wax seal, a wizened old man staggered in. The man had a long white beard that reached down to his knees, and was wearing a jet-black cloak that covered his form in its entirety.

Rising from his throne, King Adam went to greet the stranger.

When they were both seated, and once tea had been served, the old man spoke:

'O great King Adam of Zilzilam,' he said, his words muffled with age, 'I have waited seventy years to bring you a message, a message that will save your kingdom and your life.'

Adam looked into the old man's dull eyes, and wondered whether he was unhinged. But before he could say a word, the stranger went on:

'When I was a young man,' he said, 'I was a shepherd on a remote hillside a great distance from here. From dawn until dusk each day, I tended the family flocks. And, each night, I would bed down on the hay in a little stone barn, and I would sleep like the dead.

'One night, while deep asleep, I walked from the barn, over the hills, until I came to a jagged rock face. There, in a cleft between the crags, an oracle spoke to me. It said that I was to be a messenger and that, one day many years hence, a good king would be saved by the message I was to impart.'

'What was the message?' asked Adam gently.

The old man held out a withered hand.

'I shall tell you,' he said. 'Each night I would return to the crag as a dream-walker. And I would listen to the message of the oracle. And, little by little, the oracle passed on details of the message in a most unusual way. Only when the entire message had been entrusted to me did I awake to understand that I had been the confidant to an oracle.

'As the messenger, I was instructed to keep the message with me at all times in a certain way, and to bring it to you on this day. The oracle said that you, King Adam, would understand the secret wisdom held within it, and that by doing so, your kingdom would endure until eternity.'

'Could I have the message?' asked Adam, growing a little impatient.

Again, the old man held out a hand.

'I shall give it to you,' he said solemnly.

Standing slowly to his feet, he unfastened the

buttons of his jet-black cloak, and the robe fell to the floor. Beneath it, the ancient was naked.

Every inch of his skin was tattooed with words.

'*This* is the message,' he said.

And, with that, he expired.

Bending over the emaciated corpse, Adam began to read…

The Unicorn's Tear

THERE WAS ONCE a swordsmith in Shandong who devised a secret method by which to craft a blade that never grew blunt.

The more lives his swords claimed in battle, the sharper and more deadly they became.

Word of his breakthrough spread and, as it did so, every knight there struggled to get his hands on such a weapon.

As a consequence, there were more wars, battles and duels than there had ever been – as knights, warriors, cavaliers, and ordinary soldiers fought one another to get possession of the blades.

An entire generation of fighting men was slain.

Witnessing the carnage, the master swordsmith took his own life, so horrified was he that he should have been responsible for filling all the cemeteries of the land.

But the deaths continued.

Day in, day out, warriors lost their lives for no reason but to fight for the sake of fighting. And, with each death, the swords became ever sharper.

Then came the day when every knight in the land was dead.

All except for two.

The first was named Da Shun, and the second was called Fu Sheng.

They met on an isolated hilltop overlooking the sea, as the rain lashed down. Each clutched a blade that had slain a thousand men.

At the appointed moment they began swinging blows at one another.

For a full day and a night, they fought.

But so equally matched were they that neither managed to inflict a mortal wound on the other. Collapsing at the same moment on the windswept knoll, they both understood the futility of going on.

Fu Sheng spoke first:

'Neither of us can win at this,' he gasped.

Da Shun cocked his head in agreement.

'So what shall we do?'

Silence prevailed for a long while, and then Fu Sheng said:

'Let the first person to pass here decide who is the victor.'

'So be it,' intoned Da Shun.

And so they waited.

For days, and weeks, they waited.

In that time the two knights became friends. They shared jokes and secrets, and still they waited.

Until, one morning, an old crone heading towards the town passed them.

'I am going to sell my berries,' she said, 'please allow me to pass unhindered.'

Da Shun put down his sword.

'We will not harm you, old woman,' he said. 'Rather we just ask that you settle a score, and decide which of us is the winner of our duel.'

The crone didn't know much about duels and duelling, but she knew enough to know that duels took place to decide who the victor would be.

So she said:

'Fight your duel, then, and that will decide.'

'But we have done just that,' sighed Fu Sheng. 'We have fought and we have fought, and have fought, and have fought, but we are so equally matched that neither can win.'

'I see,' said the crone.

'So,' responded Da Shun, 'which is the winner? You decide.'

The woman looked at both the knights, and she pitied them.

'There is only one way to decide this,' she said.

'What is it?' asked the knights both at the same time.

'You must leave this hilltop,' she said in a low voice, 'and find a unicorn's tear. The one of you who can bring it to me first will have won the duel.'

The knights looked down at the crone and they both frowned. As knights they expected a decision to be more immediate and simple.

'Can you just choose one of us right now?' asked Da Shun. 'The loser will have to fall on his sword.'

'That's the way it's always been,' added Fu Sheng.

'I don't care how it's always been,' said the old woman.

'Very well,' replied the knights in time with each other.

And, without another word, they left the hilltop.

Clambering onto his mare, Fu Sheng rode to the north. And, mounting his steed, Da Shun rode to the south.

Many kingdoms passed beneath the hooves of each horse. Both of the knights sought a unicorn for its tear, but neither had much luck at all.

Da Shun was directed to a cave in which a magician was crouched over an iron cauldron. When he asked where a unicorn might be found, the sorcerer pointed into the pot.

'You are cooking unicorn?' he asked in horror.

The magician nodded.

'Well, where might I find a *live* unicorn?'

'Up there,' the sorcerer said softly, motioning to the sky.

'Where?'

'In the floating kingdom.'

Hastening outside, Da Shun cocked back his head and looked up into the clouds. Thousands of feet above, he spotted the outline of a city. He blinked, rubbed his eyes, and blinked again.

But the floating kingdom was real.

There were soaring turrets, domes, spiralling towers, high trees, a citadel, and impenetrable ivory-white walls. Even though it was day, stars were glinting above the floating city, for it was always night in that realm.

'How do I get to it?' asked Da Shun.

The sorcerer rubbed his hands together until they were warm. Then, touching them to the knight's shoulders, he moved his hands in circles.

Da Shun sensed something happening, something extraordinary.

Where his shoulders had been, wings were growing.

Great, powerful golden wings.

'Take to the wind and fly!' cried the magician. 'But beware. The wings will melt away as soon as you reach the floating kingdom.'

Clenching his leg muscles, Da Shun thrust himself into the air.

He flapped and he flapped, and was soon soaring high against the cobalt sky. Looking down, he spotted the sorcerer, no more than a pinhead far below. As he flapped, the skyline in the clouds came into sharp focus. Capping it was a night sky, a panoply of stars gleaming like grains of salt tossed across a dark shroud.

Da Shun rose high above the city walls, arcing

to the east. But, as he turned, the golden wings seemed to lose their might.

All of a sudden, they broke apart, and Da Shun began to fall.

He fell, and fell, and fell, plunging down into the dark.

Fortunately for him, a deep mosaic pool in the palace grounds broke his fall. Before he knew it, Da Shun was being rescued from the water by a dozen maidens. Taking him to the guest quarters, they begged him to be at ease.

'May I be presented to my host?' Da Shun asked over and over.

The reply was always the same:

'In time perhaps but, alas, our queen has left on a journey, from which we await her return.'

As Da Shun was reclining in great comfort, Fu Sheng was hacking his way through the red jungle of Salanaque.

A blind merchant had sold him a fragment of information at a distant caravanserai: that a unicorn was kept prisoner by a blue troll, a troll who lived where the red jungle bordered the eternal sea.

The merchant had declared that the troll, the most fearful of creatures, could frighten a man to death by turning its face inside out.

Chopping his way through the jungle, Fu Sheng gained no more than a few inches a day. Each night as he slept, the undergrowth ahead doubled in its thickness, making progress impossible.

His strength sapped by leeches and sores, the knight vowed not to yield until he had presented the crone with a unicorn's tear.

At last, one day, Fu Sheng noticed a breach in the radiant red light ahead. Chopping with his razor-sharp sword, he reached an expanse of empty land. In the middle of it stood a plain wooden shack.

Striding up to its door, Fu Sheng knocked hard with his fist.

The door swung inwards slowly.

A teal-blue creature was standing in its frame. He had short blue horns, a hairy blue brow, and a face so wart-ridden and foul that it sent a pang of raw fear down Fu Sheng's spine.

'I am on a quest for a unicorn's tear,' said the knight.

The blue troll took half a step backwards and turned his face inside out.

As a reflex to a sight so offensive, Fu Sheng whipped out his blade and separated the troll's head from its shoulders.

Instantly, the plain wooden shack disappeared.

Where it had stood, a palace rose from out of the ground, its crenellated walls and towers fashioned from the whitest marble. All around, the forest melted away, and was replaced by a pristine city.

As Fu Sheng stood before the palace, wide-eyed in amazement, the troll's bluish blood not yet wiped from his blade, a drawbridge lowered.

Under the portcullis rode a pair of royal guards.

'Please come with us!' one of them called out.

'The queen awaits you,' said the other.

Confused, and blathering questions, the knight was led into a vast reception hall. Illuminated by coloured crystal chandeliers, the room was carpeted in rose petals, and decorated with exquisite paintings of unicorns.

All of a sudden came the delicate sound of hooves on stone.

Fu Sheng turned, and found himself gazing

at a sight more lovely than any other he had ever imagined.

A beautiful princess was riding towards him on a silvery-white unicorn. Her hair was tied back with peonies, her dress white lace. Smoothing a hand down the creature's mane, she slipped easily off the animal's back.

'I am Queen Amberin,' she said in a kindly voice. 'And I have been returned to my kingdom as a consequence of your actions. It has been floating among the clouds, waiting for this day.'

'The blue troll...' stammered Fu Sheng.

'Yes... he placed a spell on me from which I could only be freed by a blade wielded by the heart and not by the mind.'

'So odious was he,' said the knight, 'that I slayed him before I could think.'

'And that is what saved me,' said Queen Amberin.

She smiled.

'You do not recognize me, do you?' she whispered.

Fu Sheng thought back through his many adventures.

'I am searching for a unicorn's tear,' he replied,

'and on my journey I have experienced many places and many people. Forgive me if I do not recognize you.'

The queen smiled abundantly.

'I was the crone who sent you and your duelling partner to find the tear and to bring it to me,' she said.

Fu Sheng drew a hand down over his face. He sighed.

'Then I have failed you.'

Again, the queen smiled. And, gently, she pulled something out from around her neck – a glass phial, hanging on a silver chain.

'This is what kept me safe all these years,' she said. 'A unicorn's tear.'

'But why did you dispatch us to search for it, if you had it already?' asked the knight, a tone of frustration in his voice.

'Sometimes in life the most effective route is not the shortest one,' Amberin replied. 'Through calculations and divinations I came to understand a method by which I might be freed from the troll's spell. It involved two brave knights crisscrossing the world on a quest – the quest for a unicorn's tear. Only through your quest could I be certain that the conditions would be right in order for the troll to be slain as he was, by your blade.'

'But what of my fellow knight, what of Da Shun?' asked Fu Sheng.

Queen Amberin held up a finger.

'I shall reunite you both,' she said, 'so long as you both promise to be as brothers.'

'But which of us was the winner?' asked Fu Sheng.

'Both of you, and neither of you.'

The queen clapped her hands and a secret door slid back in the east gallery of the reception hall. Reclining the other side of it in a palatial salon was Da Shun.

Before he and Fu Sheng were reunited, each one promised to regard the other as a brother and a friend.

When they had done so, their swords were melted down, the metal used to make a statue. It commemorated a wise queen who saved a life and regained her kingdom at the same time.

For many days and nights, festivities continued in the Kingdom of Salanaque.

The queen honoured the two knights, bestowing the highest title of chivalry upon them. Having been presented with royal robes, decorations pinned to their breasts, Da Shun and Fu Sheng led a grand procession down to the quay.

With trumpets heralding the moment, the knights took their leave of the Queen of Salanaque and her realm, and climbed aboard the royal galleon.

They sailed for a hundred days, across oceans and seas.

But, the night before they were hopeful of arriving home at their own kingdom, the ship was boarded by pirates. Unarmed, Fu Sheng and Da Shun were enslaved along with the crew.

They were shackled and beaten to within a hair's breadth of life, then cast into a cell block of the death camp at Oran.

No man had the energy or interest to speak. For, if the jailer heard a voice, he would open the door and slit the first five throats he could touch with his blade.

And so they existed in a dark, dank realm of squalor and silence.

But one man did have the courage to speak, albeit in a whisper.

An old sailor, he was ragged and cheerless, and his voice sounded like stone grinding on stone.

And this is what he said:

'In heat more terrible than I can describe, we sailed into a small cove far to the south, a cove nestled on the coastline of far-off Senegal. We went ashore, slung hammocks in the trees, built a fire on the beach, and cooked up some langoustines.

'I can taste their meat: all juicy and tender, with a hint of coconut and spice.

'That cove was idyllic, a paradise known only to one who has known the sea. Close my eyes and I can see the shadows thrown by the palm fronds in late afternoon, and can hear the sound of the birds gliding through the heat.

'As the evening approached, we sat round and shared stories, stories of our travels and of our lives.

'I remember it, clear as I am here with you now.

'The man beside me was a Spaniard. His name was Alfonso, and he had one of those faces you could never forget: hollow features and an expression baked through from ordeal. Drawing a little on his pipe, he stooped to stoke the fire for a moment, his eyes lost in memory.

"'I will tell you a tale," he said softly. "A tale of another time, a time when I was not a sailor, but an apprentice to a master bookbinder, in Toledo. The bookbinder was the greatest craftsman of his age, from a family of ancestral binders to royalty no less. Clients would arrive at his workshop from across Spain. Sometimes they even came from France, and beyond. And it was a Frenchman, a famous writer from Troyes, with whom this tale is concerned...'"

Finis

Afterword

Since early childhood, I was raised with the notion of a Chain of Transmission.

It's the idea that progress is made by layers of action, achievement, and thought – layers laid down through a group, or even by members of a single family. In my case, the latter was very much the focus of attention.

My father, the writer and thinker Idries Shah, devoted his life to making certain psychological and philosophical traditions available to the West. Much of the material he presented had of course been in existence there for centuries. But, more often than not, it was as though the thinking was a valuable tool, kept in a glass case – viewed with awe, but rarely actually used.

Like a relay runner in a race, my father was the one who passed me the baton, urging me to run with it, until it was my time to pass it on. He, in turn, had been entrusted it by his father, The Sirdar Ikbal Ali Shah, who'd been handed it by his own father.

This theme of a Chain of Transmission runs through my family's core, and is regarded as more important than anything else. Of greater consequence than any single member of the family, it constitutes a kind of mass Group Think... a Group Think that embraces me, my father, and grandfather, my great grandfather, and all those who came before them. It's my mother and grandmother, too, my aunts, uncles, cousins, and all the rest – forming a single unified contribution to human society, bridging East with West.

My father used to explain how, whether I understood it or not, I was part of a machinery that was laden with certain responsibilities. He went on and on about it, sometimes filling me with dread and fear – as it would any small child. I didn't understand why I couldn't be like all the other kids in the school playground, why I had to be part of a Chain of Transmission that seemed to make no sense at all.

As the years passed, and as I began to understand the world and its ingrained systems,

I learned that change takes time. Beyond that, I learned that it takes a group effort, as well as recalibration through increments.

One of the most fundamental aspects of the Chain of Transmission I was handed, and expected to pass on, relates to what you might call 'Looped Thinking'. It's the sense that by circling back over the same ground in different ways, we learn to absorb ideas. And, once we've learned to absorb, we're ready to apply what we've learned.

The reason I'm explaining all this is not to try and impress anyone reading it with what I, or members of my family, have ever been exposed to. Rather, I am hoping to pass on something else – something related to Looped Thinking and the Chain of Transmission…

You could call it 'Framing'.

As those who've read any of *The Thousand and One Nights* knows, the story is set up in a curious way. Having discovered that his queen has been unfaithful, King Shahriyar resorts to marrying a virgin bride each day, and having her executed at dawn.

This barbaric practice continues, until that is, the daughter of the Grand Vizier, whose name is Scheherazade, marries the king and begins to tell him a story... a story that at dawn remains unfinished. Intrigued how it ends, he allows his new bride to keep her throat for another day.

Each evening, the story continues... for a thousand and one nights. In that time, certain ideas, themes, and bodies of information are revisited time and again. And, as the story moves forward, certain tales spring off into other tales which, in turn, give forth to framed stories of their own.

At one point there are nine tales in play.

Imagine it...

A tale, in a tale, in a tale, in a tale, in a tale, in a tale, in a tale, in a tale, in a tale.

This framing appears as a tool in other Oriental treasuries, and has been copied throughout history. Chaucer borrowed the device for his *Canterbury Tales*. And more recently, in the 1930s, my grandfather employed it in his *The Golden Pilgrimage*. In that volume, a group of travellers thrown together at a remote caravanserai share stories, in stories.

After reading *The Golden Pilgrimage* as a child, I longed to create a looped structure that would eventually circle back to its beginning, while encompassing the kind of themes and ideas I'd been raised to pass on.

I never planned for *Scorpion Soup* to be that book.

Indeed, I never planned it at all.

One drab Monday morning, having slouched down into my office chair at Dar Khalifa, my Moroccan home, I read a grim message from an equally grim publisher, ordering me to knock out a book I didn't want to knock out.

I remember reading the threatening email three or four times, and sighing long and hard. The last thing any writer wants to do is to create where there's no creative spark.

So, having sighed three or four more times, I let my attention drift from the computer screen, over the desk, and out through the open doors of my library... into the garden.

I saw myself wandering down to Casablanca's port.

The next thing I knew, I'd begun...

...begun the tale that was to spiral down, down, down, through a series of tales, before the last line looped back to the first.

In most cases I love the writing process more than I can describe. I love the business of transforming a blank screen, or a blank page, into a document that changes the way people see the world around them. I love the raw ingenuity of the writer's craft. And I love the way a book can be a kind of Trojan horse, a container for ideas, themes, and values, all of them far more important than the characters, or the storyline.

I think it would be true to say that I loved writing *Scorpion Soup* more than any other book I've ever written – because it was a book that truly wrote itself.

As I typed, I would watch my hands from a distance, as though they weren't mine... in the same way that a puppeteer must marvel at their hands having taken on a lifeblood all of their own.

The way I see it, *Scorpion Soup* was a story that my fantastical alter ego gave the rest of me as a gift, a daydream...

... a reminder that since childhood I was charged with passing on the baton, itself a loop of collected culture – my small part in the Chain of Transmission.

A REQUEST

If you enjoyed this book, please review it on your favourite online retailer or review website.

Reviews are an author's best friend.

To stay in touch with Tahir Shah, and to hear about his upcoming releases before anyone else, please sign up for his mailing list:

 http://tahirshah.com/newsletter

And to follow him on social media, please go to any of the following links:

 http://www.twitter.com/humanstew

 @tahirshah999

 http://www.facebook.com/TahirShahAuthor

 http://www.youtube.com/user/tahirshah999

 http://www.pinterest.com/tahirshah

 https://www.goodreads.com/tahirshahauthor

http://www.tahirshah.com